RUTHLESS KING

KING

BOOK ONE OF THE MOUNT TRILOGY

MEGHAN

MARCH

Editor: Pam Berehulke
Bulletproof Editing
www.bulletproofediting.com

Cover design: @ Letitia Hassar
R.B.A. Designs
www.rbadesigns.com

Cover photo: @ Sara Eirew
www.saraeirew.com

Interior Formatting: Champagne Book Design

Visit my website at www.meghanmarch.com.

ABOUT THIS BOOK

New Orleans belongs to me.

You don't know my name, but I control everything you see—and all the things you don't. My reach knows no bounds, and my demands are always met.

I don't need to lend money to a failing family distillery, but it amuses me to have them in my debt. To have *her* in my debt.

She doesn't know she caught my attention.

She should have been more careful.

I'm going to own her. Consume her. Maybe even keep her.

It's time to collect what I'm owed.

Keira Kilgore, you're now the property of Lachlan Mount.

Ruthless King is the first book in the Mount Trilogy.

RUTHLESS KING

ONE

Keira

ARE THOSE FOOTSTEPS?

I freeze outside the door to my *locked* office and stare at the handle like it's tainted with anthrax.

My employees wouldn't dare. They know my office is off-limits. And my parents are seven hundred miles away in Florida, living it up as retirees on the monthly payments I send them from the dismal profits of the distillery. It's barely hanging on, even after four generations of clinging to life making Irish whiskey in New Orleans.

This basement isn't haunted. This basement isn't haunted.

I repeat that truth like a chant until my heart slows to a semi-normal pace. My dead husband's ghost better not be inside, or heaven help me, I'll kill Brett again myself.

Summoning the same iron will it has taken to dig

1

this company out of the trenches, I grasp the handle, yank the door open, and fling myself inside, attempting the element of surprise. Or false courage. Or . . . something.

"Trying to make an entrance?"

The deep voice that comes out of the dark chills me to the very marrow of my bones.

I've only heard it once before, through the battered wood of the same locked door I just barged past, but it was delivering threats I didn't understand, not asking a question in that cool, controlled manner.

There's no way I want to be in the dark with this voice.

He's not a ghost. He's worse.

He's the frigging boogeyman, whispered about in the shadows but never mentioned in polite company, almost as if saying his name will make him appear. And no one wants that.

I've never said it. I don't even want to think it now, but my brain conjures it anyway.

Lachlan Mount.

I fumble around, slapping the concrete wall to find the light switch, but when I flip it, nothing happens.

Oh, sweet Jesus. I'm going to die and I won't even see it coming.

My antique desk chair creaks just before the dim glow of my desk lamp clicks on.

I see his massive hands first, then darkly tanned forearms with white cuffs rolled up. The light doesn't reach his face.

"Shut the door, Ms. Kilgore."

Swallowing back the saliva pooling in my mouth at the fact that *he knows my name*, I move my hand as though directly responding to his command. I grope for the handle behind me, when all I really want to do is turn around and run.

To the police.

Maybe they could . . . I don't know. Save me?

I glance over my shoulder, clutching the knob as the door creaks shut, the urge to flee growing as the dim light of the hallway disappears from sight.

"Take a step in that direction and you'll lose everything."

My feet freeze to the cracked cement floor as a bead of sweat rolls down my chest. Normally I would attribute it to the sauna-like conditions produced by the whiskey stills, but not tonight.

"What do you want?" I whisper. "Why are you here?"

The chair groans as he rises to his feet, those wide fingers refastening the button on his suit coat, but his face never comes into the light.

"You owe me a debt, Ms. Kilgore, and I'm here to collect."

"A debt?"

My mind scrambles to think of how in the hell I could owe him money. I've never met him before. Hell, I've never seen him before, only heard his voice while I eavesdropped. My kind doesn't mingle with his—well, at least, most of my kind. A few rumors circulated that he kept Richelle LaFleur, a girl from our church, as a mistress until she went missing a year ago. I shut that path of thinking down completely.

"What are you talking about?" Somehow, I manage to form the question.

Two fingers push a document titled PROMISSORY NOTE across the scarred wood of my desk into the watery pool of light. My eyes lock on the papers, but I'm too terrified to step any closer.

Oh, sweet Jesus, Brett. What did you do? My heart slams against my ribs.

"Don't you want to know how much your husband borrowed with this place as collateral?"

"How much?" I ask, inching toward him against my will.

"A half million dollars."

I suck in a shocked breath. "You're lying."

With both hands on the desk, he leans down, exposing his face in the dim light. Hard features carved from granite, piercing dark eyes, and an unrelenting stare contrast with the relative civility of the suit that fits him to perfection.

"I never lie."

A half million dollars? No way. "I would've known if Brett had borrowed that kind of money, and let me tell you—he didn't."

He shrugs as if the information means nothing to him. And maybe it doesn't.

"His signature says that he did, and this debt is overdue."

My eyes zero in on the papers on the desk. *If he really did this . . .* The effects would be catastrophic.

Four generations of Kilgores have dedicated their

hopes, dreams, and fortunes to keeping this legacy alive. It can't end with me.

"I don't have the money."

"I know."

His response throws me back on my heels. "Then why—"

He moves out of the light and comes toward me. I shrink back against the wall as he advances, blocking my escape route to the door. There's nowhere to run. He has me trapped.

"Because there's something I might be willing to take in trade."

It takes everything I have to keep my voice steady as my heart threatens to burst from my chest. "What?"

He stops a foot from me, and his full lips form a single word.

"You."

TWO

Keira

I LOCK THE DOOR AND SAG AGAINST THE WOODEN panel as soon as it shuts behind him with a decisive click. My body trembles like I just survived an encounter with the anti-Christ. All that's left of Lachlan Mount in my office is his deceptively alluring scent—an intense burst of citrus mingled with spice and cedar—and my terror.

And I can't forget the promissory note.

My gaze darts to the desk and then away.

It has to be fake. Brett *did not* borrow five hundred thousand dollars using the distillery as collateral, because he certainly didn't use the money for any of the improvements I've been making. Every dollar that has gone into this place has been courtesy of the dog-and-pony show I put on for what seemed like every banker in town.

I'm in debt up to my eyeballs. Or, at least, I was. Now I'm in over my head.

Lachlan Mount.

I squeeze my eyes shut and lift my chin toward the ceiling, inwardly cursing my dead husband. My dad would probably say I'd be better off looking down to find his spirit.

How could you do this to me, you asshole?

This debt . . . to that man . . . is the final nail in Brett's proverbial coffin. How could I not have seen through him for the user he was? Self-recrimination floats through me for the thousandth time. It's like a bad rerun on TV I can't help let play on. I fell for his bullshit lines. Thought we were going to build my family's empire again. I thought I'd found a partner. I was the dumbass who suggested eloping because I was so convinced he was the one.

It didn't take long before I realized he was an opportunistic asshole who cheated on me since before we were even married and started skimming money from the distillery bank account as soon as he had access.

I slap my palms against the solid oak door behind me. "Fuck you, Brett. *Fuck. You.*"

I take a deep breath, open my eyes, and straighten my spine. My pity party is over. I've spent just over three months dealing with the fallout of his death, only a month longer than we were married, and just when I thought I was finally back on solid ground . . .

Lachlan Mount happens.

I glance once more at the document sitting on my desk. The desk my great-grandfather had shipped over from Ireland that he'd sat at when they'd signed the very first lease for Seven Sinners Distillery property. There'd been seven sons, and their optimism about ruling the whiskey market had been undeniable.

I thought I finally proved myself worthy of sitting behind that desk when my father agreed to let me buy him out. I was so proud to be the first woman to take the helm of a distillery producing the finest whiskey in the Irish tradition in New Orleans, where our family planted roots and came to prosper even with the bitch of a law called Prohibition.

Part of me wishes I'd been alive during those days of lawlessness. When might made right, and a man—or a woman—could rise and fall according to how hard he or she was willing to work. But then again, I could picture Lachlan Mount there too with a tommy gun, eliminating every bit of competition in his way. Except he was probably still eliminating his competition the same way even now.

Actually, I have no idea how we managed to escape his notice this long, but apparently that lucky streak is over.

I summon my ladyballs and cross the cold, cracked floor to look down on the document that sits on the desk so innocently. I reach out as though I should have a hazmat suit on before I touch it, and grasp a corner of the paper between a thumb and forefinger.

I leave as much of the legal BS to the lawyers as possible, but with their hourly rates running so high and adding up so quickly, and with barely enough money to pay the overdue bills I already have, I've had to learn plenty myself just to keep costs down.

Promissory Note.

I read it word for word. My quick-and-dirty summary: this one document spells out the doom of my family's heritage.

Brett Hyde borrowed five hundred thousand dollars from Lachlan Mount four months ago and it was due in full last week, on the three-month anniversary of Brett's death. Or, if you wanted to get more specific, the anniversary of the discovery of his remains in a burned-out car in the Ninth Ward with an unidentified female.

A cacophony of emotions riot in my chest like brass bands on opposite street corners in the French Quarter, competing for tourist dollars.

This is a disaster.

I can't pay it.

Mount knows I can't pay it.

But there's something he's willing to take in trade.

I stumble around the side of the desk as my knees turn to water, and I collapse into the chair.

"*You.*"

Shivers rip through my body, leaving chill bumps across every inch of my exposed skin, even though the leather still carries the heat from his body. Like his blood runs hotter than any ordinary man. And maybe it does. One thing is safe to say—Lachlan Mount isn't an ordinary man.

Sweet Jesus, what would he want from me?

My inner voice of reason develops an attitude. *Are you serious? What the hell does any man want from a woman? You'll pay on your back.*

There may only be a few things I know as absolute

fact in this life. Seven Sinners Whiskey is the best I've ever tasted. New Orleans will always be my home. And I am not going to prostitute myself to pay my dead husband's debts.

But still, that word hangs in the air.

"You."

My hand shakes as I flip through the pages, committing the words to memory. But, really, the only things on this paper that matter are the amount I can't pay and the date it was due. I flip it over, not wanting to look at it anymore, but a bold scrawl on the back mocks me.

Seven-day payment extension granted.

There's an illegible signature beneath it, but it doesn't take a genius to know whose it is.

Seven days? It wouldn't matter if I had seven months. I can't come up with a half million dollars.

What did Brett do with the money?

I wait in silence like the good Lord might answer me in a booming voice from the heavens, but that obviously doesn't happen.

Does it really matter at this point? It's gone. He's gone. And I'm the one left on the hook because as I unpleasantly learned, as the sole beneficiary and executor of his estate, all his debts became mine to deal with. The mess of a bad marriage lasts a hell of a lot longer than *till death do us part.*

I will not roll over and pay for Brett's bad decisions on my back.

The steady thrum of fear running through my veins attempts to weaken my titanium spine.

"I will find a way to fix this. Somehow. Some way. I will."

The silence in my office is the only answer I need.

I don't believe myself either.

But I have to do something or I'm fucked. And, apparently, Lachlan Mount will be doing the fucking.

THREE

Keira

I APPROACH MY LIFE LIKE A GENERAL. A TACTICIAN. Each decision researched and executed with precision. My father always said I should have been a surgeon, but the only thing I ever wanted to do was make whiskey. He wanted a son to carry on the family tradition, but he got three daughters instead, and I'm the only one who cared about the difference between single malt and single barrel.

Right now, I need information on a man who lives in the shadows, so I go to the most obvious source—Google. I type in his name, and in less than a second the following message appears on my screen.

> YOUR SEARCH – LACHLAN MOUNT –
> DID NOT MATCH ANY DOCUMENTS.

That's impossible. I click on the image tab and it's blank. I add New Orleans, and dozens of sites pop up with information about the city, but nothing about Lachlan Mount shows beneath the preview of each.

I try a dozen more searches, all providing the same result.

It's like he doesn't exist. Like he truly is the myth and legend I thought he was before I came face-to-face with him yesterday.

So, how the hell am I supposed to get any information on him if he's a ghost where the Internet is concerned?

Last night, I tossed and turned as the minutes and hours ticked down to my deadline. My tiny apartment doesn't have a money tree growing out back, so it's safe to say I'm no closer to a solution than I was before.

I could sell a kidney, but even that's not going to get me $500,000, I assume. It's not like I stay up on the black-market value of organs, because, well, I'm a normal, law-abiding citizen.

I sell whiskey. I pay the excise taxes that make me want to vomit when I write the check. But I don't cut corners. I play by the rules.

As I walk in through the side door of the distillery, heat from the three massive pot stills surrounds me. Others would find it stifling. To me, it provides a sense of comfort. It's home.

Louis Artesian, my head of distilling operations, lifts a glass to the light before sniffing and tasting.

"How's it coming along?"

He swings his head around with a grin stretching his lips. "Mark my words, Keira, this is going to be the best we've ever produced."

The smile that tugs at the corners of my mouth isn't forced. It's pride. *I will make my father proud.* I took a risk by changing grain suppliers—without telling him, I might add—and it's going to pay off huge.

If I can keep the distillery open long enough to bring it to fruition.

All night, I worked through scenarios. When I signed the loans with the bank, it was all based on the assumption that every loan was already disclosed. I didn't know about the debt to Mount. How could I disclose it? And if it wasn't filed with the state and on record, then it doesn't count, right? Or could he be second tier and force a foreclosure to get what he's owed, after the original lenders are paid off? It's not like I know the ins and outs of any of this stuff, and what's more, I assume it doesn't matter. I can't imagine Lachlan Mount abides by the normal rules that apply to everyone else.

There's only one person I know who might be able to give me some insight. And since Google failed me, she's my next best option. No general makes decisions without information.

"Don't you think, Keira?"

Louis has been speaking to me, and I've completely zoned out. "Sorry, what?"

His kind smile reminds me of all the people whose livelihoods depend on me.

"No matter. I was just saying you made the right call. It was a ballsy move going to the organic grain, and a costly one, but this speaks for itself."

Any other time, my lungs would heave a sigh of relief, relaxing my stiff posture, but not today.

I can answer honestly, however. "That's the best news I've had all week."

"Keira, can I borrow you for a second?" Temperance, my overworked and underpaid assistant / right-hand woman calls from the doorway. It's a running joke that she works at the distillery, given her name. "We have a few more decisions to make for the event that I don't want to commit to without your approval."

In addition to being my right hand, Temperance has also taken the lead on a massive Mardi Gras event we were lucky enough to snag—one for the New Orleans Voodoo Kings, a local pro football team. They're renting out the entire restaurant, and the money coming in will be enough to keep our head above water for a few more months. At least, it would have been until . . .

I shove the thought of my unexpected and unwelcome visitor out of my head and give Louis a thumbs-up before walking toward Temperance, leaving the heat produced by the stills behind.

"What's going on?"

"They want to upgrade the menu to include something Odile is pissed about. They also want us to co-ordinate a car service, and police all the attendees to make sure none of them leave with their keys in hand to drive drunk. Bad PR, you know?"

The thought of having to be the one to tell a professional athlete that he isn't sober enough to drive home—and possibly take his keys—sounds like a nightmare.

"So, basically, they want *us* to be the bad guys? Why

can't the team do it themselves if they're so worried?"

"I don't know, but they said this has to be added to the contract or they'll hold the event somewhere else."

Oh, hell no. We need this event.

I think fast. "Tell them yes. But tell them we'll have to set it up as a mandatory valet service, and that we need someone from their organization at the door with one of our people to make it a joint decision."

Temperance pulls out one of three pens she has anchoring her dark brown bun before scribbling on her notepad with it. "Okay, I'll see if they bite on that." She glances up. "And if they don't?"

"Give in, but tell them we're only doing it for public safety reasons and reserve the right to call the cops if someone gets rowdy."

She adds the note to her list. "And about Odile—"

"How much is their request adding to the price of the menu?"

Temperance flips the pages on her notepad. "Our food cost goes up by ten percent. I haven't given them a quote on the change."

"Tell them it's a thirty-percent increase in the cost, and when they push back, settle on twenty-five. And then tell Odile I owe her."

Temperance's grin widens as she scribbles. "See? You're a born negotiator. This is why you rock at your job."

If only I could negotiate my way out of a certain debt.

I'm saved from discussing anything further as my phone vibrates in my hand. I glance down at the name on the screen.

This can't be a good sign.

"Sorry, I have to take this," I tell Temperance.

"Of course. I'll catch up with you later on any other details. This is going to be great for Seven Sinners. Also, I have a line on a few more organizers interested in reserving the space for events, and a couple other ideas that could really be profitable. I'll fill you in tomorrow."

Normally I'd be thrilled to hear this, but I'm already distracted completely by my caller.

"Thank you, Temperance. This is why *you* rock at your job." I stride down the hallway.

"Hey," I answer.

"You know I don't get up before noon. You better explain these cryptic-as-shit texts that woke my ass up," Magnolia Marie Maison says.

After Magnolia dropped out of Sacred Heart in tenth grade because her scholarship got pulled, my mother told me I couldn't see her anymore. The ban wasn't surprising, because Magnolia got caught giving our history teacher a blow job in the supply closet. Mr. Sumpter disappeared, but Magnolia viewed the situation as finding her calling.

Mama tried to exorcise her from my life, but that's not how friendship works, at least in my book. Magnolia is the one who beat up Jill Barnard when she made fun of my pixie cut in fourth grade, which also resulted in a suspension. She coached me through using my first tampon. Took me to the clinic to get birth control after I got asked to prom at a boy's private school, because she swore she wasn't going to let me make any stupid mistakes with my life.

Magnolia is the big sister I never had. The one who looked out for me and always made sure I stayed out of trouble. My loyalty to her runs deep, and in my opinion, how she makes her living is no one's business but her own.

"Mags, I have a problem."

"What, you getting hit on by another restaurateur who only wants to carry Seven Sinners if you have a private dinner to talk it over with him?"

I can practically hear her rolling her eyes over the phone. That has been the extent of my male interactions since Brett died, and she knows it.

I duck into my office and shut the door behind me before I speak. "Lachlan Mount. He was here." As soon as I say his name, the goose bumps return, along with the lingering seductive scent he left behind. I'll probably have to fumigate my office to get rid of it.

Magnolia's voice goes quiet. "The fuck did you say?"

"Lach—"

"Shut your damn mouth and do not say that name again."

My teeth clack shut.

"He is not a man you want to know you exist. And we can't talk about this over the phone. I'll get up. Get dressed. *Fuck.*"

Her reaction validates everything I've been thinking. This situation isn't bad. It's catastrophic.

"What do I do?" I hate the fear making my voice unsteady.

"You get your ass to my place and tell me every

damn thing that happened. Bring some of that whiskey of yours too, because we're gonna need it."

"I have a full day of meetings—"

"Ke-ke, your schedule just got fucking clear. Get your ass to my place."

Magnolia ordering me around usually is more along the lines of "Ke-ke, take that shot. Don't be such a pussy." Or, "Just go out and get some dick, for the love of all that's holy. Your cooch is gonna dry up."

Depending on the circumstances, I ignore those comments. This order, I can't ignore.

"I'll be there in twenty."

"Make it ten."

I park my twelve-year-old Honda Civic in a guest space of the parking garage of the poshest new condo complex in New Orleans. It's full of cars worth at least ten times the value of mine.

And while Mama disapproves of the path Magnolia has taken, no one can argue it hasn't been a lucrative one. She holds the distinction of being one of New Orleans' most exclusive madams, and the details of how she got there have never been shared with me. Everything I know came anecdotally, including the fact that her little black book of johns is *thick*. And what's more, Magnolia has the dirt on just about all of them, or so she claimed on the night when we celebrated me taking the helm of Seven Sinners.

As I slip out of my car and shut the door, careful

not to ding the Porsche parked beside it, my breathing speeds up. Magnolia won't pull punches. She'll tell me just how screwed I am.

I cross the pristine parking garage floor to the elevator and press the call button. It appears instantly, and within moments, I'm standing in front of the entrance to her sixth-floor condo. She hasn't quite reached penthouse status, but I have no doubt she's heading there. Magnolia has as much entrepreneurial spirit running through her veins as I do, if not more.

Maybe that's part of the reason we're kindred spirits. We're both in the business of sin.

She opens the door on my first knock, and her peach silk dressing gown emphasizes her every gorgeous curve. Instead of the normal smile I usually get when I show up, she grabs me by the arm and yanks me inside. She slams the door behind me and locks the dead bolt.

I face her, a lump growing in my throat. "It's bad, isn't it?"

"Where's that whiskey you brought? We're gonna need it."

I pull a bottle out of the Tory Burch bag she gave me the night we celebrated, and hold it out. Magnolia grabs it from my hand and carries it to the counter as I follow.

"There are things in my world that should never cross into yours, Ke-ke. You're sweetness and light, despite the fact that you make badass whiskey. But you crossed into it, and I have no fucking clue how we're gonna get you out of it whole."

She reaches up and snags two crystal tumblers off glass shelves in the bar area and splashes whiskey into them, three fingers each.

Magnolia is always confident, bold, and never shows any kind of hesitation. The fact that her personality has taken a one-eighty kicks up my heart rate until it hammers in time with the tapping of her long peach acrylic nails on the counter.

"What do you mean?" I ask slowly, because I have a feeling I'm going to need an explanation that's just as slow.

"You've been marked, girl."

"What does that mean?" There's no way to disguise the fear edging my words.

"I did some digging."

"How? I just told you—"

She cuts me off with a hand in the air. "You know I can get to the bottom of a mystery faster than a crack whore can find the bottom of a dime bag. Don't act all surprised. This took one discreet phone call, and what I found out isn't good."

I reach for the crystal tumbler and gulp down the single malt that any other day I would sip and savor, noting the flavors as they caress my palate. Not today. Today, I need liquid courage to face whatever is coming out of Magnolia's mouth next.

She leans both elbows on the counter and drags one long, glitter-tipped nail around the rim of the glass. "Lachlan Mount is not someone you fuck with."

"I didn't!" I sound like I'm on the verge of hysterics, and to be honest, I am.

"Nothing happens in this city without his say-so. He's like a conduit through which all things must pass. Booze. Drugs. Girls. Cons. Gambling. How the man amassed so much power, I have no idea, but he did and he holds it with an iron fist." She looks up at me. "Now you're in his grip."

"Booze? We've never paid him off."

"You sure about that?"

"I would've known. Dad never mentioned—"

Magnolia tilts her head to one side and then the other. "Doubt he would. Hell, maybe he's kept paying him off since you took over to keep him away from you. Doesn't matter now. You owe him, and you can be sure he's gonna collect."

I can't imagine my father paying off Mount regularly, and I have no idea how I'd even begin to bring up the subject. The implications hit me hard, and I watch the color drain from my face in the mirror behind Magnolia.

"I don't even know what Brett did with the money. I didn't know he borrowed it in the first place."

Magnolia's gaze drops away.

"What? What aren't you telling me?"

"Ke-ke, you know I love you, but there are some things you don't need to know."

It doesn't surprise me that Magnolia would try to shield me if she could, but right now, I need answers. I take a slow, deep breath and let it out, as though preparing for something painful. Which I suppose I am.

"Tell me what you heard."

After a few beats, she finally speaks, her tone flat.

"Word on the street is that part of the money went to pay off one very irate loan shark, which is like borrowing from the devil to pay one of his minions. Some went to his very expensive nasal problem, and the rest to the bitch he was banging on the side, because she told him she was pregnant. That's all rumor and hearsay, though."

My knees are supposed to hold me up, but they fail. I fumble for a grip on the counter, but miss and fall flat on my ass on the floor. The crystal tumbler shatters on the marble as I go down.

"Ke-ke!" Magnolia bolts toward me, her arms outstretched.

I hold my hands out. "Don't. Just. Don't."

Stunned, I suck in breath after breath as I process her words.

Loan shark.

Nasal problem.

Pregnant mistress.

I knew Brett was cheating on me. He barely tried to hide it. I can't even believe it took me almost the entire four months we were married to figure it out. It's why I met with a divorce lawyer three days before he died and leased an apartment so I'd have somewhere to go when I filed the paperwork.

Magnolia backs away and reappears with a broom to sweep up the broken glass. I pull myself together and stand. There's one part of what she said that doesn't make sense.

"What kind of nasal problem did Brett have? Allergies?"

She dumps the dustpan in the trash bin and looks at me with an expression that can only be described as sympathetic. "Ke-ke, he was a cokehead. Since before the day you met him."

"What?" The word bursts out of me. She surely can't mean . . .

"Cocaine. Blow. White."

"That's impossible. I would've known. I—"

"You're a good girl," Magnolia says, shaking her head benevolently. "You can recognize a drunk at twenty paces, but drugs are out of your wheelhouse, Ke-ke."

"That piece of shit put my family's legacy at risk because of *drugs*?" I'm no longer on the verge of hysterics. I'm there.

"That and pussy, which is even more addictive, in my experience. Plus, Brett Hyde was a con artist. He had you hook, line, and sinker before you even had a chance."

I cover my face with both hands and focus on breathing. Counting to ten. Trying to let the anger recede.

It doesn't work.

Eloping with Brett was the one impulsive decision I've made in my life. I thought meeting him was fate. He was so perfect for me from day one, I couldn't help but believe the world had destined us to be together. And after that incredible night . . .

I shake off the memories. I was such a naive little idiot.

"I wish I could bring him back to life so I could

kill him myself," I whisper.

Magnolia aims another indulgent smile my way. "Sweetie, if he were still alive, you know I'd chop off his pathetic excuse for a dick with a meat cleaver."

"What the hell am I going to do?" I ask her as I begin pacing the marble floor.

Magnolia's head swivels back and forth as she watches me. "Ke-ke . . . this shit is serious."

I spin around to face her. "I know. I need five hundred thousand dollars or I'm fucked. How the hell do I get a half million dollars in a week? No bank in this town will loan me another cent with the debt I already have."

She clasps her hands together in front of the silk belt knotting her peach robe closed. "I'm gonna get real with you. Even if you were a virgin, there's no way we could organize a payday like that so quick."

I squeeze my eyes shut. *Auction myself off?* A shudder of disgust slithers down my spine. *Even that's not an option because I'm not worth that much.* I look up and meet her tawny gaze.

"Brett got five hundred thousand in a week. I have to be able to do it too."

"No one is gonna give you that money." Her face is solemn.

"What about another extension? A payment plan?" I jam my hands into my hair as I attempt to think of all other possible options.

"Girl, you don't need me to tell you that isn't gonna solve your problem."

I cross my arms over my chest, hugging them tight

around me before walking backward until my knees hit Magnolia's leather sofa and I land on it.

"What if . . . what if I just don't pay? What if I tell him that it was Brett's problem and he's dead, so leave me out of it?"

This time, Magnolia's gorgeous golden face pales. "Keira," she says, and I stiffen when she says my full name because she *never* says my full name. "You don't want to go down that road."

"I don't have a choice! I don't have the money."

Magnolia crosses the room slowly and sits on the couch next to me. "The last woman who crossed Mount ended up in the morgue."

Goose bumps prickle every inch of my skin as I swallow. "He killed her?"

Magnolia's slow shake of her head sends an icy rush of fear into my veins.

"Mount doesn't have to do his own dirty work anymore. But that bitch was sliced and diced. Died from blood loss."

I picture a woman bleeding out in a dark alley, slit from ear to ear, but Magnolia continues.

"They say his people pumped her full of uppers and forced her to dance barefoot on broken glass until eventually she fell and managed to grab a shard. She slit her wrists herself just to end it."

My stomach rolls as I picture the brutality in vivid color. I bolt off the couch with my hand over my mouth, making a mad dash to the bathroom.

Magnolia is behind me in moments, pulling my thick red hair away from my face. "I shouldn't have told you. But I don't know how else to make you understand what you're dealing with. You don't want to know what I heard they did to her boyfriend. It was even worse."

I heave again, bile burning my throat as I retch. Magnolia rubs my back until I wipe my hand across my mouth.

"Water?" The request comes out as a croak.

"Sure, hon."

I follow her out of the bathroom, back to the kitchen, picturing the broken crystal shards she'd swept up moments ago, except this time I imagine them digging into the soles of my feet as my blood stains the floor.

Magnolia slides a bottle of water across the counter to me, its cap already removed, and I take a cautious sip.

"What am I going to do?"

She covers my free hand with hers. "*We,* sugar. Because if you don't give the man what he's owed, then he won't stop with you. He'll take out everyone you love."

I gag on the sip of water. "Oh Jesus, I have to leave. I can't get you involved—"

"Too late. Mount never makes a move without knowing everything about his target."

"My parents . . . my sisters . . ."

Magnolia nods. "And your friends. Employees."

My eyelids sink closed. "He said . . . he said there was something he was willing to take in trade." I hate to voice the option, but I can't contemplate the alternative consequences without running for the toilet again.

"What?"

I swallow another wave of rising bile before I answer. "Me."

"Well, fuck."

FOUR

Keira

"WHAT?" I ASK, TERROR RUNNING RIFE AT her whispered curse.

"I'm thinking." Magnolia holds up a hand.

"Has he done this before? Is there a playbook for this?"

She shakes her head. "No. I mean, the man has had plenty of mistresses. He usually orders them from out of the country."

"And?"

"After a few months, they disappear. Like they never existed to begin with."

I think of Richelle LaFleur, the girl we knew from church that no one has seen or heard from again and was rumored to have been one of his mistresses. As far as I know, the police consider her disappearance a cold case.

My breathing speeds up again. No matter which

way I look at the situation, the only ending that seems to be consistent is me dying.

Magnolia eyes me carefully, as if studying my every feature for the very first time. "After that mess with Richelle, he hasn't been with any local girls."

"Why deviate from his pattern now? Why me?" My words come out sounding just as frenzied as my brain.

Magnolia shakes her head. "God only knows." Her reply doesn't make me feel any better about the situation. She steps away, crossing to the counter to grab her cell. "I need to make a phone call."

She leaves me on the couch as she walks out of the room, and I draw my knees up to my chest and contemplate my options. Magically come up with five hundred thousand dollars. Prostitute myself out to a man who has either killed or ordered people killed, and everyone he sleeps with disappears afterward. Or, prepare to die a horrendous death, knowing my friends and family are going to die too.

All because of Brett.

How could I have been so stupid? We'd met online, my first foray into the world of Internet dating. We'd been ridiculously compatible. Our first date had been a dream. It was effortless, the way I thought real love should be. And our chemistry? Off the charts. At least, at the very beginning. I was the one who brought up eloping, and he said it was the most romantic idea he'd ever heard. So, we did it.

And he was a con artist.

I thought he'd been so interested in the distillery because it was my passion, and after we got married, he wanted to be part of running it. We were going to be an unstoppable team, and that thrilled me. Until I spotted him and the other woman. All of a sudden, his reduced interest in sex with me became utterly apparent. He was too busy fucking someone else to want to go another round with me.

It was time to truly face the facts. Brett Hyde conned me. He never wanted to be part of a team. He wanted to use the distillery as collateral for a half-million-dollar debt to a man scarier than any villain Hollywood has yet to create.

I can't stop picturing a woman dancing on shattered glass until the pain was so horrendous she slit her wrists.

He's a monster.

I squeeze my arms tighter around myself, and Magnolia returns a few moments later.

"I only have a hundred liquid. I could borrow another two, maybe two and a half from my connections, but I can't pull together five hundred in a week."

I blink twice and stare at my best friend until I realize she's talking about giving me the money. "I didn't come here for that. I couldn't take—"

"Of course you wouldn't come here with your hand out, because that's not the kind of girl you are. But I would give it up for you if I could. Your ass isn't on the line by itself, sweet thing. If you default, we all go down with you."

Yesterday morning, I woke up feeling like I normally do—determined to take on the world of whiskey and make Seven Sinners the household name it has never been. Today, I'm worried about whether I'll be alive in another week.

All because of Lachlan Mount. *No. Because of Brett.*

"I already told him I don't have the money. He knows."

Magnolia nods, her teeth skimming her lower lip. "Doesn't surprise me at all. The man knows everything that happens in this town. What does surprise me is that he's willing to take pussy for payment on a half-mil debt."

I cringe at her crass language, but one thing I've always respected about Magnolia is she calls a spade a spade.

"I've heard of him taking property, houses, boats, racehorses, and cars, but never a woman. This isn't his normal behavior."

The gears in my brain turn slowly, as though rusted together from information overload. "Why deviate from the pattern?"

Magnolia tilts her head to one side and studies the wreck I surely am. "Have you looked in the mirror lately? I mean, when you weren't puking your guts up?"

I roll my eyes.

"Ke-ke, you are *shit hot.* I could book you out every night of the week and twice on weekends."

"I know you mean that as a compliment, but—"

"But nothing. You got tits, ass, and that gorgeous red hair that makes a man think he's gonna find fire when he gets you under him. And don't get me started with those eyes of yours. You've cornered the market on untouchable class. And what's more, you're totally and completely oblivious to it."

"Brett clearly didn't think so." I don't even know why I say it. Reminding myself my husband was cheating on me sucks more every time.

"Brett was a fucking tool and never deserved you. And right now, you need to quit worrying about him and start worrying about Mount."

I unwrap one arm from around my chest and pinch the bridge of my nose. "I don't even know where to start."

Magnolia cocks a hip to the side. "I have a feeling he'll be calling all the shots, so it won't matter either way. Actually . . . maybe that's what'll save your ass. From what I've heard, the others were all meek and submissive—"

I jerk back into the couch cushions. "That's definitely not me."

She holds up a hand. "No shit. And maybe that's it. You're full of fire and sass to match that ass of yours. You gotta use it."

I don't like where she's going with this, and my belly flips in agreement. "I seriously have no idea what you mean. At all."

"When you're Lachlan Mount, no one defies you. No one gives you sass. Something about you caught his eye. I feel that in my bones. You have to use it. Work it. Don't let him walk all over you." Magnolia's voice quiets. "Don't let him break you, Ke-ke. You keep ahold of your pride and never let go. He won't know how to handle you."

The thought of Mount *handling* me turns my

stomach again. "There's really no other way? No other client—" I can't even believe I'm throwing the option out there as a possibility.

Magnolia destroys my last hope with a shake of her head. "You've already been marked. Lachlan Mount owns your ass, regardless of whether he's tapped it yet. No one else will touch you because they'll want to keep their limbs intact."

"He gave me a week. I have to find another alternative."

"That's the part I've been trying to figure out. Normally, when a debt to Mount is due, *it is due*."

"Can't I go to the police? Won't they do something?"

Magnolia looks toward the ceiling, as though seeking patience from a higher power. "*Please* tell me you're joking. Because if you take one step in that direction, we're all dead."

"So you're saying . . . I have to do this."

She lowers her gaze to mine, and I feel the grimness of her stare. "You don't have a choice. Not another one you can live with, anyway."

"And you want me to defy the man who's never been defied?" I cough out a strangled laugh. "Are you trying to get me killed?"

She shakes her head again, biting her lip as she holds up a finger. "No. I'm trying to save you."

"Fuck," I whisper. Because honestly, what else is there to say in this situation?

"But there's one more thing you gotta watch out for, girl."

I don't want to know where she's going with this,

probably down some other dark and gruesome road, but I have to ask. "What?"

"When you've got as much power as Mount, that much charisma, that much *presence*, it does things to people."

"You're losing me."

"Listen to me, Ke-ke. Hear me." Her sharp tone clues me in to the fact that this is no joke. "He's going to make your head go to war with your body."

My heart kicks up again. "I don't understand what you mean."

Magnolia lets out a long sigh. "I'll put this in plain terms. You're gonna tell yourself that you don't want him, that you hate him, and that this is all happening against your will. But there's something about that man that tells me he's gonna fuck with your head and turn your body against you. Mark my words, Ke-ke. He will make you *enjoy* it. He will make you *want* him."

The gravity of her stare presses me back into the couch. "No way. No *fucking* way." I jump up, my arms at my sides, my hands fisted.

"Yes fucking way. Get this through your head." She comes toward me and wraps a hand around my arm, her nails digging into my skin. "There's no shame in enjoying it, if that's what's gotta be done. My girls do it all the time. Drop-dead gorgeous client, one they'd fuck for free? Doesn't even feel like work."

I stiffen under her grip. "I'm not one of your girls." The words come out from between gritted teeth.

"But you're still female, and chemistry isn't something you can fight." She surveys me with knowledge in her eyes I can't begin to imagine. Her grip on my arm loosens. "Just . . . be careful. He's not like any man you've ever met. But whatever you do, don't show fear. Don't let him fuck with your head. You're strong. Hold on to that. But if you enjoy it . . . what's the harm?" She releases her hold on me with a shrug.

"No way in hell."

FIVE

Keira

I DON'T REMEMBER ANY OF MY DRIVE HOME.

I should have gone back to work. The fundraising event needs to be locked down, and I should be asking for details on the other inquiries we've had. But I can't. My brain won't focus, and I find myself parking in my spot at my run-down apartment building instead. When I realize where I am, I call Temperance and tell her I'm not feeling well. It isn't a lie, by any means, and not just because I puked my guts up at Magnolia's.

I refuse to believe there's only one way out of this that doesn't end with everyone I love dying. But any way I look at it, life as I know it is over.

"After a few months, they disappear. Like they never existed to begin with."

Mount can't make me disappear. I have people who would notice and then scream bloody murder if the cops didn't look hard enough. I'm not some random girl from a foreign country, or like Richelle with no family left to keep the case alive after the police shelve it.

When I open my door and climb out, a BMW pulls to a stop along the curb across the street.

Is it following me? Or is it just another random nice car, and my mind is playing tricks on me? Either way, the fact that I can't see through the black-tinted windows puts me on edge. I hoist my bag onto my shoulder and lock my car door.

My keys jangle in my shaking hand as I walk with uneven steps toward the front entrance. When I let myself inside, I glance over my shoulder at the car, but no one gets out and the window doesn't open.

Ignore it. It's nothing. And regardless, from the way Magnolia described things, Mount would have no reason to have me followed if he already knows everything about me.

That knowledge makes me feel stripped bare, even though I'm fully clothed.

Unless they're watching to see if I'm going to run.

I make my unsteady way up the stairs to the third-floor apartment I leased the day I met with the lawyer and planned to file for divorce. My townhouse, the one Brett moved into the day we got married, is a rental and the lease is about to lapse. I planned to renew it. At least until . . .

I push the memories of that day from my mind and focus on getting inside. I could have picked a nicer place to crash-land after my divorce, but I already planned to cut my salary to the bone to keep up with the distillery debt.

My parents sold their place when they moved to Florida, so that wasn't an option. When they flew home for Brett's funeral, Dad was pissed when he learned I planned to move into what he called a *shithole*, but I made up some excuse about it being closer to work and not needing so much space anymore as the reason for letting the lease lapse. I couldn't admit that I didn't think I could afford to pay myself enough to stay in the townhouse or find a better apartment. I wasn't about to admit how badly we were struggling.

Knowing my dad, he would have insisted on coming out of retirement to take over, but that was the last thing I wanted him to do. Not just because I want to be the one at the helm, but because I feared he'd have a heart attack when he realized the damage Brett had done and how close Seven Sinners teeters on the edge of failure.

All my parents knew was that Brett had cheated, I was leaving him, and then he died in a tragic accident before I could file for divorce. As a compromise, I let Dad install two new dead bolts on my shitty apartment door. That was three months ago, and everything since is a blur.

I took it one day at a time, making sure all the bills got paid, and settled Brett's affairs. With the big payday from the fundraising event coming soon, I thought we would finally have some room to breathe.

But no.

Now things are even worse.

My fingers itch to pick up the phone and call my dad for guidance, but I know I can't. If what Brett did would give Dad a heart attack, what Mount suggested would cause heart failure. And if it didn't, he would show up with a shotgun and try to hunt Mount down, and based on Magnolia's information, we'd all be dead.

So, I will not be telling my parents, and I sure as hell won't be telling my little sisters. Imogen is finishing her PhD, and Jury is partying it up somewhere exotic, working behind or on top of a bar somewhere, just enough to fund her playgirl lifestyle.

My decision is clear—my family can *never* know about any of this.

I drop my bag on the worn blue velvet chair in my living area and stride toward the kitchen, intent on finding another bottle of whiskey since I left the other with Magnolia.

I'm halfway across the tile floor when I freeze.

A copy of the promissory note is on the counter. I know it's a copy because the original is in my bag.

He was here.

Torn between making a run for it, but remembering the car parked outside, I snatch the document off the chipped Formica. Something metal pings off the tile as another piece of paper floats to the floor.

I scan the faded tile and stained grout, not seeing anything but the note with two words written in a bold hand I recognize immediately.

Six days.

I leave the note where it is, fighting another shiver of fear as I drop to my knees to search for whatever else he left.

I crawl toward the coffee table and something glints in the afternoon sunlight near the edge of one leg. I dive for it, but my fingers shake so violently I can barely pick it up.

No way. Impossible. It can't be.

I hold the circle of gold up to the light and read the inscription inside my dead husband's wedding band. Ice water takes the place of blood in my veins.

How? Why?

I bolt for the chair, grab my bag, and lunge for the door. When I've finally unbolted it, it swings open and I'm ready to sprint for my car.

Until I crash into a solid male body.

I look up, expecting to see Mount, but it's not. Why would he bother with such a menial task if he's busy running an empire?

Instead, it's my super, Phil.

"Everything okay, Keira?"

I want to scream *nothing is okay*, but I shake my head and mumble, "Fine. Great. Thought I forgot to lock my car. Gotta go check it."

Phil nods. "Can't be too careful in this neighborhood."

He moves on down the hall and I lock my door behind me, although part of my brain is wondering why I do it when it's clear locks aren't a deterrent to Mount or whoever he sent.

When I burst out of the building, my gaze shoots across the street. The black BMW is gone, and in its spot is a silver Prius.

Was it Mount in the BMW? Or someone who reported to him?

The words on the note flash in my head.

Six days.

The only thing I'm going to figure out in six days is how to drive myself completely crazy.

Once I lock myself in my car and jam the key in the ignition, I inhale deeply and release the breath slowly, attempting to calm my hammering heart.

My instincts scream at me to run, but where the hell do I go?

Mount was in my office at the distillery. He was in my apartment. Nothing feels safe anymore.

Maybe that's part of his plan? He wants me helpless, like I have no options. Weak. Powerless. Under his control.

You've underestimated me, Mount. You might get me, but I won't come cowering before you.

In my shitty Honda Civic, I make a vow to myself.

I will not run. I will not hide. And I sure as hell won't put anyone else I care about in danger by bringing that monster to their doorstep.

I yank the key out of the ignition and get out of my car and lock it again, retracing my steps, feeling steadier with each moment. Once I'm inside, I find a bottle of Seven Sinner's single barrel in the cabinet and a glass. I set everything—both versions of the promissory note, Brett's wedding band, and my six-day warning—out in front of me.

Tonight, I'm going to reread every word of my death sentence, and then I'm getting drunk.

SIX

Keira

GOING TO WORK WITH A HANGOVER SUCKS, especially when you're the boss. In this case, I had no option. Passing out was the only way I was getting any sleep last night. It took a bottle and a half of whiskey to do the trick. High tolerance and all.

As I go through the motions, my employees pretend not to notice that something's off with me. Even Temperance gives me a wide berth and doesn't mention anything about the fundraiser.

By lunchtime, I feel like I might finally be able to stomach food, and I climb the stairs to the top floor of the distillery where we have an incredible restaurant whose fare is surpassed only by the excellent 360-degree view of the city. I designed the remodel after I saw pictures of the Gravity Bar at the Guinness Storehouse in Dublin, not that I've had the pleasure to go there myself.

With Brett's debt and Mount's threats hanging over

me, maybe now I never will.

The lunch crowd in the restaurant is light. I nod at a trio of businessmen, and make small talk for a few minutes with a couple of ladies who ask about my mom and how my folks are liking it in Florida.

"They say they're never coming back, but we'll see."

"Living the good life. It's so wonderful they were able to keep the business in the family and still retire. It's tough to manage that these days."

"It really is." I force a smile onto my face. "Have a wonderful lunch."

When I duck into the kitchen and smile at Odile, our head chef, she shakes her head.

"I'll have someone run your regular down to your office. No reason for you to wait in my hot kitchen while I make it. You got me catering to whatever those fancy rich people want for their event; no reason I shouldn't be catering to you too."

"You are a goddess, and those fancy rich people keep us all employed."

She responds with a *pshhh*. "You do that by force of will alone. It's that stubborn Irish in you. Now, you need to learn how to use the phone and call up to place an order like I would expect the CEO to do."

I can't tell her I had to get out of my office because Mount's scent still hangs in the air, and every time I close my eyes, I picture him sitting behind my desk or trapping me in the corner.

"Tomorrow. I swear."

I skip the elevator again in favor of the stairs. It's basically the only exercise I get, and the elevator takes me longer to get back to the basement.

I'm not sure about other distilleries, but in my family, the basement office signifies that the CEO learned the business from the bottom up, and serves as a reminder to always stay humble and grounded.

I've always loved the basement for that reason, down to the faint scent of mildew that clings to the old wooden beams. But now it feels foreign and forbidding.

When I reach my office, I feign my familiar confidence as I reach for the doorknob, telling myself there's no reason to fear going inside. But as soon as I open the door, I'm proven wrong.

My desk lamp was off when I left, and now it's on. In the pool of light is another note.

Five days.

Beneath it is the framed picture of my sisters and me that normally hangs on the wall behind the desk.

My instinct is to freeze in terror *again*, but instead I force out a declaration from between gritted teeth.

"You don't scare me, Mount. I refuse to cower."

This time, there's no answer from the darkness.

The notes keep coming.

Four days, with a picture of Magnolia and me from Sacred Heart taken in ninth grade. It was left on the front seat of my locked car.

Three days, with a copy of the picture of my

employees and me from our company newsletter. This one is rolled up and stuffed in my employee mailbox.

Two days, with a snapshot of me *in my own freaking restaurant*, tacked onto a box of copy paper in the storeroom across from my office.

One day, with a photo taken from a distance of my parents on the golf course wearing the same clothes they'd had on in the selfie they posted on Facebook *yesterday*. I found it in my purse, which I keep in the locked drawer of my filing cabinet, when I needed my credit card earlier.

Mount made his point, and I'm about to go crazy waiting for whatever is going to come next.

I throw down my pen, unable to concentrate on a damn thing, even wistfully reading the itinerary of the Global Whiskey and Spirits Convention I won't be going to next week in Dublin because Seven Sinners can't afford extra pens, let alone such an outrageous expense. Maybe next year. If I'm still alive.

I'm sick of waiting. Sick of wondering. I pick up my phone and call the only person I can talk to about this disaster. "How do I find him?"

It's not a request, it's a demand, and Magnolia is quick to reply.

"You don't find him, Ke-ke. He finds you."

"But he sent me a picture of my parents that was taken *yesterday*."

"I told you this guy doesn't fuck around." Her voice is quiet.

"Well, I'm sick and tired of waiting. I'm done. *Done*. If he wants me, then he's going to get me, and I promise he's going to wish he hadn't."

Silence hangs in the air for a few beats. "You need to simmer down with that redheaded temper you got going on, girl. This isn't a game where you get to make the rules. I told you how it works. He calls the shots or—"

"Or people die," I say, interrupting her. "I get it. He made his point, and I'm *done*. I want it over with. Just tell me where the hell I can find him."

"Ke-ke—"

"Don't tell me you have no idea, because I won't believe you."

Her sigh is long and put-upon. "I don't know for sure, and that's not a lie. But I have heard if you go to a very specific bar on Bourbon and you give a very specific code word, someone will vet you and you might be taken to him—*if he wants to see you.* It's like the queen of England; you can't just demand an audience."

"He better want to see me. That's what he wants right? Me?"

"Think about this before you do something stupid. The bar and code-word shit is all rumor and hearsay, and for the record, I wouldn't try it if I were you. Just wait. You've got one more day and he'll make his move."

It's like Magnolia hasn't known me since I was ten. Patience has never been my strong suit.

"No. No more waiting. I'm going on the offensive. Tell me where I need to go and what I need to say."

"This is a bad idea, Ke-ke."

My heart pounds as a lump rises in my throat, almost blocking the words. Maybe it's my common sense trying to intervene. *Too bad.* I swallow and make my demand one more time.

"Just tell me, Mags."

For a few beats, I don't think she's going to tell me, but she finally rattles off the information.

"Think about what you're doing, girl. This isn't a bear you want to poke. You have a lot of people on the line here, and I'm not saying that to be selfish. I'm prepared to meet my maker any day of the week, but I'd just as soon prefer it not be today."

I suck in a deep breath and exhale slowly. "I'll let you know what I decide." I disconnect the call before she can try to talk me out of it again.

Lowering my cell to the desk, I stare down at the promissory note that has ruled my every moment for the last six days. The promissory note that will make me into a whore to pay my cheating bastard of a dead husband's debt.

A gurgle of hysterical laughter escapes my throat. It sounds so ridiculous. I never bought into the bullshit concept that life is supposed to be fair, but how is it right that this was dished out on my plate? I think back to the time I heard Mount's voice, when he was in this very office speaking with Brett. It wasn't the date they signed the note, that's for certain. It was after.

Maybe they argued about payment?

I wish I'd been a better eavesdropper for once in my life, because maybe I'd have some kind of ammunition for when I face the devil in his lair.

All I can remember is the murmur of Brett's voice and the anger in the stranger's tone. That doesn't help me at all. So, now I have the name of a bar and a secret password. Practically speakeasy-style straight out of New Orleans during Prohibition when my great-granddaddy was selling bootleg whiskey to keep the family fed.

Kilgores have always done whatever it takes to survive, and that trait carried through to me.

But does survival mean waiting one more day, or going to track him down?

I heft my purse over my shoulder and walk out of my office, still uncertain of my course of action.

SEVEN

Keira

I DECIDE TO WAIT A DAY BEFORE DOING ANYTHING crazy. After that, all bets are off because it's D-Day. *Due day.*

"You want me to tattoo *what exactly* on your ass?" The bearded giant stares at me with more shock in his eyes than I would have expected for a New Orleans tattoo parlor by the name of Voodoo Ink.

"It's not like you care, is it?"

He leans forward, resting his thick, inked forearms on the counter. "Look, lady, for starters, I'm booked out for the next six months solid."

I cross my arms and stare at him like I'm not impressed, but I actually am. *Who knew this place was so good?*

"It can't take you more than fifteen minutes to do it. You have to be able to fit that into your busy schedule."

Someone laughs from the back, and heels click against the black-and-white checkered floor toward the

50

front of the shop. A gorgeous woman with Bettie Page bangs dyed bright blue assesses me.

"The only reason a woman wants PROPERTY OF NO MAN tattooed on her ass is because of a bad breakup."

"The kind of breakup that ends with a cheating husband dead in a burned-out car in the Ninth Ward?" I eye them both, my chest twinging to put it out there so heartlessly, but facts are facts.

The man pushes off the counter, and the woman's eyes widen. Their changed demeanors make me think they know exactly who I am now. Brett's death definitely made the eleven o'clock news.

"I'm afraid we won't be able to help you today, and I have a feeling most of the other shops in town are going to give you the same response," he says, his rough voice a little softer.

The woman steps around the counter. "How about we go grab a cup of coffee next door, and you can do that 'spilling your guts to a perfect stranger' thing to get it off your chest without making a terrible mistake of getting a bad tattoo you'll regret for the rest of your life."

It's on the tip of my tongue to tell her the rest of my life probably won't be very long, but instead I follow the swish of her retro pink dress, with black crinoline peeking out from beneath the skirt, as she leads me out of the tattoo shop.

The coffee place next door is really a donut shop called Your Favorite Hole. I've never stopped there because every donut I eat goes straight to the ass I wanted tattooed, and it's already a tight fit in most of my jeans.

The woman orders for both of us, not bothering to ask me what I want. The barista whips into action, serving up the drinks in record time with a bag of donut holes.

"That one's for you." She nods down at one cup and takes the other and the donuts to a table.

I pick up my drink and follow her.

"I'm Delilah, by the way," she says, holding out her free hand.

"Keira."

"Kilgore, right? I figured after your story. Not many people can duplicate that mess. But, honestly, I thought I recognized you before. You make bomb-ass whiskey. I love the single malt, and that cocktail you make with lemonade and a sprig of mint. Seriously, to die for." She pauses. "And for the record, I'm really sorry for your loss. No matter what, that sucked."

For some reason, the latent urge to cry rises, but I shove it back down. Brett has already gotten more than enough of my tears.

Instead, I simply say, "You have no idea how much."

She takes a sip of coffee before lowering it to the table. "I believe you. So, are you going to tell me what spawned the tattoo idea? Because you'd be surprised by how many good stories I could tell you that start with us refusing to tattoo someone's ass."

For a single moment, I consider spilling the story to her of the disaster I'm in, but I can't risk dragging another innocent person into the fray. Or more accurately, the killing zone.

"Maybe I just feel the need to declare my independence," I say vaguely.

"Which implies you feel like someone is trying to take it from you."

I shoot her a sharp look for her astute observation. "Are you a tattoo artist or a counselor?"

She laughs and digs into the bag for a donut hole. And good Lord, do they smell delicious. Cinnamon and sugar and all that delicious pastry. I'm tempted to grab one, but hold myself back by sipping the coffee. It tastes a lot like the smell of the donuts.

"I'm a little of both most days. I've seen a lot of shit. Heard a lot more shit." She scans the room as though checking to make sure no one is eavesdropping before she continues. "I know you don't know me, but I'm going to give you a piece of advice. I'm assuming you've found yourself in a not-so-good situation, especially given the car with the blacked-out windows parked across the street, and the guy who's pretending not to watch you."

I start to turn my head in the direction of the front windows, but she stops me by tossing a donut hole at my face. It bounces off my forehead and distracts me.

"What the hell?"

"Don't look."

My head starts to pound, so I suck down more of the caffeine, hoping it'll kill the brewing headache.

"Okay, fine. What's your advice?" I ask as I set my coffee back on the table between us.

"While you might want to assert your independence, or perhaps send a very strong message to someone, I'd suggest finding another way to do it that's a little less permanent than an ass tattoo. I'm not kidding when I say you're going to regret it forever otherwise."

Even though she told me not to look, I nonchalantly lift my coffee again and knock over the bag of donut holes so they spill onto the table. With Delilah distracted, I take a peek.

Sure enough, there's a man in a suit leaning against a lamppost with a newspaper tucked under his arm. A black BMW is parked in the spot in front of him.

Delilah catches on to my game. "I said don't look."

"Does it really matter?"

"That you're being followed and now you know, and he knows you know?" She shrugs. "I don't know. Depends on who you're dealing with."

I drop my gaze to the lid of my coffee, playing with the flap on the cup.

"Shit. It's bad, isn't it?"

All I can do is nod.

"How backed into a corner are you?" she asks.

I pin her with a stare. "Why do you care?"

"We tend to pick up strays at Voodoo, and while I would never consider Keira Kilgore of Seven Sinners Whiskey a stray, today you seem a little less composed than I would've expected given your reputation. But if there's anything I can do to help, just tell me."

"There's nothing anyone can do to help. I mean, unless you're independently wealthy with boatloads of extra liquid capital." I grab a donut hole and shove it in my mouth to stop myself from saying any more.

As I chew, Delilah studies me again. "Fine, don't tell me, but if you really want to do this, I can recommend a good henna artist only two blocks away."

♛

I leave the henna shop feeling like I regained a shred of control over my life.

Debt or no debt, at least it's clear now—semi-permanently—that I'll never be any man's property. That wisp of positivity carries me all the way home, only to be doused by a cold rush of fear when I open my bedroom door and find a box on the bed.

No insignia or logo, just a big, shiny black box that's the perfect size to hold an assortment of severed limbs.

Good God. When did I start thinking like this?

My inner voice doesn't bother to respond because the answer is obvious. It's not like there's any doubt in my mind as to who it's from.

I grab my phone and call Magnolia.

"Please tell me you didn't do anything stupid," she says in lieu of a greeting.

"Nothing irreparably stupid."

Her sigh of relief comes through my speaker. "You didn't go try to find him?"

"No, but I'm staring at a box on my bed that he or his people clearly left."

"What's in it?"

"I haven't opened it."

"What the hell are you waiting for, girl?"

"What if there are body parts inside?"

She's silent for a beat. "You haven't tried to run. You haven't done anything stupid. There's no way he's sending you body parts. Open the damn box, Ke-ke."

That she so matter-of-factly lists those circumstances as being the reason I *haven't* received body parts reminds me just how serious my situation is. My little jaunt to the henna shop seems beyond ridiculous now. *At least they wouldn't tattoo me at Voodoo . . .*

"I don't want to open it." My tone sounds stubborn and willful, like a child who won't eat her vegetables.

"Don't make me come over there and do it myself because your stubborn little Irish ass won't. Put me on speaker, put the phone down, and open the damn box."

"Okay, fine." I toss the phone with the speaker engaged on my gray-and-white coverlet and reach for the top of the box to lift it off.

"You're not screaming, so I presume we're good on the body-part angle?"

The fact that Magnolia can be so glib about this situation is beyond me, but it's another indicator that her life and mine, at least before this last week, are totally and completely different.

"There's tissue paper. It's black."

"Well, flip that shit open, girl. I'm dying of suspense here."

I fold back the paper, and beneath it is black silk fabric that slides through my fingers like water. I lift out a dress that has to cost more than my car.

"It's a dress. Short and black. Silk, maybe?"

"Better than a body part. Much better. Bet it's expensive too."

I can't imagine a man with Mount's reputation taking the time to choose what he wants me to wear while he collects on his debt. He probably didn't. Maybe he has a personal shopper for these situations.

I check the size. Of course it's right. I start to ask how he'd know, but I remember that they've clearly been in my apartment more than once. And then I realize the name on the tag. *Versace.* Jesus. This thing is definitely worth more than the Honda.

"So, what else?"

"Hold on. I'm getting to it."

I lay the dress on the coverlet and find more tissue wrapped around a sheer black lingerie set encrusted with tiny crystals that sparkle like diamond dust.

What if they are diamonds?

I remember reading about the bra that was solid diamonds, and I've definitely walked past windows of stores selling gorgeous lingerie, but I've never bothered to go inside because I could barely afford half a thong.

Seeing this, *owning* this, should fill me with excitement, but all I feel is burning rage and building resentment.

"I hear more tissue. What else are you finding in there?"

"Lingerie."

"Of course. Bet it's the good stuff."

"It probably costs more than my rent," I mumble as I unwrap another tissue-covered object in the corner.

"And shoes." I lift one black crystal-encrusted stiletto and survey the icepick-like heel, and the delicate straps that will wrap up my calves.

"What kind?"

Of course she'd want to know.

"Manolo Blahnik." I definitely never thought I'd own a pair of these either. And now I can't even enjoy them because I'm wearing them because he has decreed it.

"Damn, girl. He went for the good stuff. I'd take that as a good sign."

The knot in the pit of my stomach disagrees with her completely.

"Anything else?"

I lift out the other shoe to find a note at the bottom written in the same black scrawl as all the others.

A driver will collect you at 9 p.m.

I read it to Magnolia.

"You best let me go and start getting ready. You need to knock him *dead*, Ke-ke. Fuck with his head instead of letting him fuck with yours."

I think of my stop earlier today. "I'll do my best." Another thought slams into my brain, and I choke out a few more words. "If . . . if anything happens to me, will you tell my parents and my sisters—"

Magnolia cuts me off. "You're not going to die tonight, baby. I swear. Give that man what he doesn't even know he wants—which is everything that's you—and you'll be just fine. Now, get going. Put that armor on and go slay yourself a dragon of a man."

I hang up the phone and stare at the array of couture spread out on the bed. I should feel like a princess getting dressed for a ball, not a prisoner on the way to her execution. But no princess ever faced off with Mount. At least, that I know of.

I pick up the note.

There's no signature. No instructions or orders to wear the clothes provided. Nothing beyond the simple piece of information stating what time I'll be *collected*. The word itself stokes the fire in my veins.

This man is so completely used to getting what he wants, he would never expect anything less than full compliance with his orders, explicit or implied.

Screw him.

Everything in me implores me to rebel. Then there's the tiny sliver that screams, *Throw a few things in a bag and run to the airport and get on a plane to Madagascar.*

I close my eyes and think of the pictures I've received over the last week. My sisters. My parents. Magnolia. My employees.

The image of a woman dancing on shattered glass. The nightmares that would become reality if I don't comply. Running would be the ultimate act of selfishness, and I'm better than that.

Mount can take his pound of flesh, but that's all he's ever going to get from me.

EIGHT

Keira

I WATCH FROM BETWEEN THE SLATS OF MY BLINDS AS a black car pulls up in front of my apartment building at nine o'clock exactly. I'm torn between wishing he was late, and knowing I don't need any more time to contemplate what the outcome of tonight might be.

Do I go out? Wait for the driver to come up? It's not like I have experience with this type of situation. No protocol from Emily Post applies here.

I already know they can get into my apartment, so why make it easy for him? I wait inside like a girl whose date just honked the horn, urging her to come out so he doesn't have to come to the door. That happened only once to me, and my father wouldn't let me set foot outside the house. No, instead he went outside to scare the hell out of the boy and school him in proper manners. Needless to say, I didn't get asked out a lot after that.

The clock on my microwave ticks over to 9:01, and still the door to the car hasn't opened. In fact, it doesn't open until 9:03 and an expressionless man in a well-fit-ting suit unfolds himself from the front seat.

He doesn't lock what has to be an exorbitantly expensive car, especially in my questionable neighborhood. For a moment, I assume he's an idiot, and then it occurs to me that I'm the idiot. If Mount is everything people say he is, then no one in their right mind would dare steal his car.

I wait another minute until there's a knock on the door to my apartment. I tighten the belt on my light-weight black London Fog trench coat, a bargain I snagged at Costco for under forty bucks. It's probably a mockery of all the expensive couture Mount sent me, but I don't give a damn.

With a steadying breath, I flip the locks and open the door.

The man gives me a quick survey from head to toe, and then jerks his head to the side. He says nothing at all, just turns and stalks down the hallway to the stairs.

I squeeze my eyes shut and step one stiletto-clad foot into the hallway, knowing that when I return, *if I return*, I will not be the same woman I am right now. This experience will change me irrevocably, and I al-ready hate Mount for that.

Although my sense of safety in my apartment is nonexistent, I take my time locking both dead bolts before following the silent man to the stairs. He walks down them slowly, as though he knows I'm not used to wearing heels this tall. The harsh fluorescent light on the ceiling highlights the jagged scar on the left side of his face. It's old, clearly, but it didn't heal well.

Did Mount do that to him?

When we reach the ground floor, he opens the front door and once again jerks his head, as if he wants me to go first.

Responding to his silent command, I pick my way down the cracked sidewalk in the skyscraper heels as Scar walks silently behind me. I don't need to hear his footsteps to know he's there. I can feel him.

When I reach the curb, I freeze as some statistic runs through my head about how unlikely you are to survive an abduction once the kidnapper gets you in the car.

The thought of running bursts into my mind again, this time lit up in flashing neon lights.

But every reason that stopped me from packing that bag for the airport follows, along with the more practical reason. There's no way I'll get far in these heels if I try to run.

What would be the consequence for that act of cowardice? I don't want to know.

Scar opens the back door for me, not even gesturing for me to get inside. It's a fait accompli. No one disobeys his boss, and he knows it.

I duck my head and slide inside the most luxurious vehicle I've ever seen. The plush tan leather seat hugs my body as he shuts the door.

This is it. My mouth goes dry at the realization.

I'm nothing more than the trade Mount demanded being delivered. I'm not even worth a single word from my driver as he folds himself into the driver's seat and starts the engine.

Based on the thundering beat in my chest, I'm certain I'm going to die of a heart attack before the car moves an inch. I swallow, but my dry mouth makes it nearly impossible.

I look down to the cupholder discreetly tucked into the interior. In it is a bottle of Bling H2O. I've never seen one in person, but I remember reading an article online about how an enterprising entrepreneur turned Tennessee spring water into a $40 per bottle product by putting it in a frosted bottle with Swarovski crystals.

Bling seems to be the theme of the night, like the water was picked to match the shoes and lingerie. Or maybe Mount is just that rich that he doesn't care about throwing money away on ridiculous extravagances.

Leery of what may be in the water, I skip the bottle and notice Scar holding something out to me from between the seats.

A black cloth hood. It looks like something put on a terrorist before the CIA drags him off to be waterboarded.

Jesus. Effing. Christ.

If I thought a heart attack was imminent before, the likelihood just increased a dozen times over.

Scar holds it out and says nothing.

Do I rebel or do I comply? That's the question I'll likely be asking myself all night.

I answer the question quickly in my head. I'm going to save my rebellion for the man who deserves it. That is, if I can summon the courage when the time comes.

"Fine," I snap, and yank the hood out of his hand

and pull it over my head.

It's not like I spent an hour doing my hair. I refused to give Mount that much consideration. My red mane was wild from me running my fingers through it all day as I freaked out about the night to come, and now it'll be even more of a mess.

I tell myself I don't care.

Once my vision descends into blackness, Scar starts the engine and silently maneuvers the car onto the street. I listen to the outside noises, all my other senses heightened as I try to figure out where he's taking me.

Traffic seems to get heavier as horns blare, and I can hear music in the distance.

The French Quarter? Is he taking me to the bar Magnolia told me about? The one with the code word? I have no way of knowing unless I yank this hood off, and I have a feeling that won't end well for me.

Twenty minutes later, there's a scraping noise and the car turns before slowly moving forward again.

A garage? A warehouse? I have no idea.

Scar kills the engine, and his door opens. A moment later, a brush of cool breeze hits my legs and I tighten the belt on my trench coat.

When a hand lands on my arm, I practically jump out of my plush leather seat. "Give a girl warning next time, okay? Do you want me to die of a heart attack before we get to wherever the hell we're going?"

He doesn't answer, just helps me out of the car while I remain blind. I expect him to pull me behind him slowly so I don't trip, but instead he lifts me into his arms like a groom on a wedding night.

The thought twists in my stomach as I remember Brett carrying me over the threshold of my townhouse after we eloped.

That lying, cheating piece of shit.

Rage roars into my veins again, stiffening my spine with the steel I'll need to face the scariest man in New Orleans.

I try to keep track of the twists and turns and going up and down, and the sounds of doors opening and things sliding, but I'm completely discombobulated by the time Scar lowers me to my feet again.

The first scent to hit my nose is a faint mixture of cigar smoke, leather, and old books. Footsteps recede, and there's another, almost silent, sliding sound. If I hadn't been blind, I might not have heard it.

I yank the hood from my head, my eyes adjusting to the dim light as adrenaline dumps into my bloodstream.

Fight or flight.

I'm ready.

I expect to see a smug man waiting for me, the one who sat at my desk like he owned it, but there's no one.

I spin in a circle, barely keeping myself upright on the tall heels. I'm completely alone.

My first thought—did Scar bring me to the wrong place? I expected a bedroom fit for a bordello with a massive bed where Mount would force me to do whatever sick things his twisted mind desired.

But there isn't a bed in sight. In fact, the only furniture in the room is heavy bookcases lining every wall, two large leather chairs perfectly suited for the frame of a big man, a few lamps on the tables, and a sideboard with crystal decanters. My eyes scan the room from wall to wall, looking for the door.

Another shot of fear courses through me when I realize *there isn't one.*

I swallow again, my mouth even drier than in the car, and focus on my breathing. *This is New Orleans. Hidden rooms and secret passageways are run of the mill. It's no big deal.*

Except when the man you're meeting has a history of making his mistresses disappear.

But that's not what I am. I'm just the piece of ass he's taking in lieu of payment for a debt. Nothing more. Nothing less.

I stand in the center of the room, waiting, and I see a dark glass bulb tucked into one corner of the ceiling.

A camera.

Is he watching me?

A shaft of courage, bolstered by my rage, straightens my spine once more.

For the first time in my life, I sure as hell hope Lachlan Mount is watching. I untie the belt of my trench coat and let it fall to the floor.

NINE

Mount

THE MEETING WON'T END. TWO TOP CARTEL LEADERS vying for power in my city sit on the opposite side of my desk. They've been arguing all evening, and I've let them.

Anywhere else, this would end in bloodshed, if they would have even agreed to be present in the same room, but they wouldn't dare here. If they want to do business in New Orleans, they go through me or not at all.

I already know what deal will be sealed before they leave the room, because I decided yesterday. I don't care that the Mexicans think they're all powerful. In my city, there is only one king, and that's me.

Rule with fear, but gain respect through actions.

That's what I've done for almost twenty years since that piece of wisdom was imparted upon me by a dying cartel jefe the CIA set up for retirement in New Orleans. He also sparked the fire in my veins that resulted in me seizing control of an empire.

After that, my life became something I could never have imagined.

CIA. NSA. FBI. DEA. ICE. Cartels. Mafia. Yakuza. Bratva.

Now I work with them all, and the most important thing I've learned is power is the only thing that matters. Most men have too many weaknesses to hold on to it for long.

V steps into the room and nods at me.

The anticipation I've been holding at bay all night rises to the surface, and I shove it down.

The Mexicans continue arguing, and in my boredom, I allow my gaze to wander to the monitor on my desk showing various camera angles, specifically the room where I had V take her.

Would she be frantically searching for an exit? V didn't text that there were any problems with the pickup. No indication she'd resisted.

There she is. She rips the hood from her head and her wild red hair spills free.

I tear my eyes from the screen and drag them back to the Mexicans as they argue some more. I listen with one ear, interjecting as necessary to keep it somewhat civil, but I find my gaze drawn to the screen again.

She hasn't started yanking books from the shelves to find a way out. That's at least interesting. But she's a fascination that will lose its luster just as fast as any other.

After a few years at this level, everything ceased to become a challenge for me. I've been bored for nearly two decades, but I'm hoping one fiery redhead provides at least some diversion before I lose interest.

I'm ready for this meeting to be over. They've drawn it out long enough.

I study the men across my desk with disgust. Two of the most feared men in the Mexican drug trade, and I could execute both of them in my office and no one could touch me for it.

When you gain the reputation of having no limits, no weaknesses, and are willing to flood the streets with blood, people don't test your boundaries or break your rules.

Part of me is disappointed that Keira Kilgore didn't put up more of a fight. I thought that Irish redhead temper of hers might come roaring to the surface, but apparently not.

Definitely disappointing.

I turn my attention partially back to the discussion, at least until she turns to face the camera directly, like she's found the lens and knows I'm watching her.

Her expression fills with defiance as she reaches for the belt of that ugly-as-sin trench coat, and I watch with rising interest. When she whips it off her body, dropping it to the floor, my cock twitches against the silk lining of my suit pants.

Fuck.

Me.

A smile tugs at my lips.

Maybe she's not a disappointment after all.

She's also completely stolen my attention from the conversation happening in front of me, which is unacceptable.

I will make myself wait.

It doesn't matter that she's standing stark naked in my library, wearing only the high heels I sent, her head held high and proud.

She will wait. Business always comes first.

Then she turns, stealing my attention once more.

My dick jerks again as she gives me a clear view of that perfect peach of an ass I now own.

At the bottom of her back, in the tramp-stamp region, are block letters that I don't recall seeing mention of in any of the information I'd gotten on her, and certainly not in any of the photos.

With a flick of my wrist, I click the frame and zoom in, ignoring the argument in front of me completely.

A growl fills my throat and fire burns in my gut as I make out the words.

PROPERTY OF NO MAN

Keira Kilgore, you are definitely no disappointment after all. Let's see how long that lasts.

She's officially shattered my concentration, which is something she'll pay for, but this meeting is over. I stand.

"Gustavo, you take the heroin and weed. Eduardo, you get the coke, pills, and meth."

Both men jerk their heads in my direction.

"But—"

"Do you want to see your mistress tonight, Gustavo? Because if another goddamn word comes out of your mouth, I will put a bullet in your head and send her your dick in a box."

His teeth clack shut, and I look to Eduardo. "Any complaints?"

"No. My organization will make it work."

"Good, then we're done here."

My eyes snap back to the monitor and the woman whose arms are crossed behind her back, both middle fingers extended.

My nostrils flare.

No man would dare. Not even these two bastards in front of me who have hung bodies of innocents from bridges in Mexico for no more reason than to instill fear.

It seems my original instincts about Keira Kilgore were right. There's a fire burning in her that I've never found in another woman.

It's time to see my latest acquisition.

TEN

Keira

I'S NOT A BOOKSHELF THAT MOVES; IT'S THE fireplace. It spins like you'd see in a movie.

I jerk around to catch it turning, dropping my hands to my sides as the man who has been starring in my nightmares for a week steps into the room. The fireplace rotates again to return to its original position.

He's even bigger than I remember from my office, but the tantalizing citrus and woodsy scent is the same, except this time it's mingled with that of the leather and books.

His dark hair, cut perfectly in a style I'd call *don't fuck with me*, matches his nearly black eyes. Those eyes seem to burn like coals as they make a lazy perusal of my naked body.

Before, when I first dropped my coat, I felt bold. Full of rage. Anger. Disgusted with my husband for putting me in this position. It gave me false courage, and adrenaline raced through my veins.

Now, reality is setting in.

I'm facing down a man who could end my life easier than I could squash a mosquito.

His full lips twist into an expression I suppose I could call a smile, but it's not. It's too smug and self-assured. Like he's amused at my expense. *Which he probably is.*

I wait for him to speak, but he doesn't. His inspection of me ends with his gaze spearing mine. I want to look away, but I can't.

His presence surrounds him like a physical being. It's meant to inspire fear, and it's doing the job. I don't know how to properly describe the feeling, except I imagine I'd feel the same way if a massive alligator were about to snap its jaws shut on my head and drag me under into the swamp. The death roll would come next. I can't let him get to me, or I'm screwed.

When Magnolia described the power, the presence, and his charisma to me, I didn't understand what she was talking about. I'm starting to now.

Don't show fear. Don't show fear. It becomes my mantra as I wait for him to speak.

After what seems like an eternity, he utters two words in a deep, gravelly voice. "Turn around."

When I deliberately flashed my backside to the camera in the corner and then flipped it the double bird, I figured there was maybe a fifty-fifty shot he was watching. Again, that insane stunt was fueled by adrenaline, which has deserted me.

I want to dredge up the remains of my rebellion, but I can't.

I spin on the stilettos, the only items of clothing he sent that I deigned to wear, and give him my back. I hold my shoulders stiffly and with pride.

Don't show fear, I repeat to myself.

The wooden floor creaks as he takes a step toward me, coming close enough that his body heat radiates against my skin.

"You don't follow instructions well."

The words ghost along my skin as his fingers spear into my hair and close around it. He tugs just hard enough to turn my head to the side, forcing me to meet his dark gaze.

It's like looking into the eyes of the devil.

How such a cruel man can be so brutally beautiful, I have no idea. My heart slams as his eyes narrow on me.

What seemed like such a bold and defiant act now seems like a childish prank, and my inner self-talk takes a 180-degree turn. *Screw not showing fear; now's the time to beg. He's going to kill me.*

But my mouth doesn't receive the orders sent by my brain and it opens, spilling out words I didn't plan to say. "You didn't give me any instructions. The note said a driver would collect me at nine. That was it."

His dark eyes flash. "You don't strike me as stupid enough to miss the implication of thirty grand worth of clothes on top of the note."

Thirty grand. Holy shit.

Again, words fly from my mouth without my permission. "That better not get added to the debt."

One corner of his full lips quirks up in what would

appear to be a smirk from anyone else, but from him, I don't know what to call it except chilling.

He releases my hair and takes a single step back. "Bend over. Fingertips to your toes."

"What?" I blurt out the question, my shock evident in my tone.

Mount's expression hardens. "I don't repeat myself for anyone."

I squeeze my eyes shut, desperate to break his stare. What did I think was going to happen? He'd whisk me from this gorgeous library to a bed where he'd make love to me and make sure I came? Something my ass-hole of a husband didn't bother to worry about 98 percent of the time.

"Do not make me wait." The words come slowly but still carry the crack of a bullwhip.

I swallow any reply and bend over, touching my fingertips to my blood-red toenails.

Blood red. It reminds me of the woman he made dance on glass.

Instead of fingers or some other appendage being jammed inside me, a callused fingertip drags along every letter I had inked onto my back.

"Property of no man. Is this permanent?"

"No," I whisper. "It's henna."

"Good, because we both know your ass belongs to me, and I'd hate to have to remove each letter from your back."

The implication that he'd carve them off with a knife is there, but he doesn't voice that piece.

Thank you, Delilah and Giant Man from Voodoo

Ink. I probably owe you my life right now.

On that ridiculous thought, I start to rise, but Mount's wide palm flattens on the small of my back with enough tension to push me back into position.

"I didn't tell you to move. The faster you learn that you do what I say, the easier this will be for you." Wry humor enters his tone. "Hell, you might even enjoy it."

Rage, like the kind that pushed me in my every action before he entered the room, fills me again. "Rape? Who enjoys that?"

His touch is gone from my skin as quickly as it came, leaving behind nothing but the heat from his skin.

"Stand up. Face me."

He barks out the orders and I follow them, finding the courage to meet his gaze. If I thought I felt rage, the same emotion is mirrored in his eyes.

"I'm going to fuck you like you've been begging a man to fuck you your entire life. And I guarantee while I'm buried inside you, there won't be a single second when you feel like it's against your will."

"Not a chance in hell. I'll *never* be willing."

The challenge I throw out hangs in the air between us as he reaches for me again. I flinch as a fingertip skims along my jawline, following the line of my throat, stopping between my breasts. My nipples peak despite my resolve.

"Your body betrays you."

"It's cold in here."

"Lie to yourself all you want, Keira. But tell me the truth about one thing. When was the last time you were fucked by a real man? Someone who knows what you need. Someone who'll take control from you and give you what you've been dying for. How many times did you have to fuck yourself with your fingers after your limp-dick husband rolled over, just so you would get to come too?"

I hate that he knows that. "Leave him out of this."

Mount's eyebrows go up. "He's why we're here, isn't he? He couldn't satisfy his debt, and he sure as hell couldn't satisfy his wife."

One finger flicks my hard nipple, and I suck in a harsh breath. He cups one breast and drags his thumb across the center, sending flames streaking through me. I want to hate it. I want to hate it more than I've wanted to hate anything in my entire life, but he's right. Magnolia was right too.

My body is betraying me.

Heat burns around us, from his hand where he touches me, from his gaze where he pins mine, and from the inferno building inside me. His thumb and forefinger close around my nipple and squeeze, tighter and tighter, until the line between pleasure and pain blurs and my thighs clench together.

He releases me in an instant and steps away like he hasn't almost just made me come from that simple touch. His head tilts to the left as he surveys me.

"You know what else power is, Keira? An aphrodisiac. You can fear me and still want me at the same time. It will heighten every experience."

My jaw clenches. I hate that there's a possibility he could be right. "I don't want this. I didn't ask for this, and I will *never* submit willingly. I swear it on everything that's holy."

His lips twist into an expression I can't read. *Fascination? Intrigue? Challenge?*

"Then you sign over one hundred percent of Seven Sinners to me right now." He steps away and reaches into the breast pocket of his dark suit and produces a single sheet of folded paper.

I cross my arms over my chest, suddenly feeling every inch of my nakedness. "No. That company is *mine*. My family's legacy. It's the only thing I've ever wanted for as long as I can remember. And if you believe I'm dumb enough to think it's only worth half a million, you've misjudged me completely."

His eyes narrow. "With your debt load? Mortgaged to the hilt? You're lucky I'd be willing to take it on and keep it running rather than shut it down and sell those stills for scrap."

The thought of Seven Sinners being dismantled sends another wave of fury washing over me. "Don't you fucking think about touching my company. I'll never let you have it." My reply can't be called anything but a sneer . . . except maybe for stupid.

I expect him to rage at me in burning anger, but he smiles smugly instead.

"I'll think about touching whatever I want." He pulls a pen from his other breast pocket. "But if you sign this, you can walk away without me touching every curve of your body until I know it better than my own. Without me sucking on those pouty pink nipples. Without me burying my hand in your wild mane of hair and using it to pin you down while I fuck that perfect peach of an ass until you scream my name."

I struggle to draw in a ragged breath as he lays both the sheet of paper and the pen on the table like a dare. The lamplight illuminates the title of yet another legal document whose only purpose is to ruin my life.

COMPLETE AND IRREVOCABLE ASSIGNMENT OF
OWNERSHIP INTEREST

Even as the fire he started rages through my body, I hate him.

Hate.

It's not a word I truly understood until just now. But by putting me in this impossible position, he's made me understand it too well. The feeling is visceral, twisting my stomach in rage strong enough to douse the flames.

"You know I won't sign that. Seven Sinners is mine. A Kilgore has run it for four generations, and I won't be the one to let it leave the family."

His smug expression morphs into burning heat. "The only way Seven Sinners stays yours is by you becoming willingly *mine*. Complete, voluntary submission. This is a one-time offer. Take it or leave it, Keira. You won't receive a more generous one from me, and you sure as hell won't receive any offers from anyone else."

I can't even look at his smug face, so I spin around and begin to pace. *Fuck being naked.* He already knows he owns me.

"That's not even a real choice, you bastard. Anyone who knows me could give you my answer in a second. I believe in my family. Our legacy. Our whiskey. Our tradition. My employees." My voice shakes as I seal my own fate and spin around to face him. "I won't sign it. You win."

I want to see the triumph on his face so I can use it to fuel my hate later when I allow him to defile my body.

His dark eyes rake over me with the heat of victory. He reaches for the sheet of paper and tears it in half, letting both pieces fall to the floor.

"I knew I wouldn't need this."

That bastard. He played me. Gave me a glimmer of hope and crushed it.

Mount crouches to grab the trench coat off the floor and tosses it at me. "Cover yourself up. You're now the property of Lachlan Mount, and I expect you to act like it. Get those words off your skin before I see you again. I don't want to read those lies while I fuck you from behind."

Property. That's how he views me. As a toy to be owned and used.

I catch the coat and jam my arms through the sleeves, buttoning it up and knotting the belt tight. This time, I keep my attention glued to the floor.

His polished black leather shoes come into view as his fingertips grip my chin, forcing me to meet his stare. "Your orgasms belong to me. If you ever touch yourself without my permission, I will spank that pussy of yours until you're begging to come."

What kind of barbaric—

I yank my chin from his grip, no longer caring about my personal safety. He's already staked his claim. What else could possibly happen? Besides, if he thinks I'm going to make this easy . . .

I stride in the direction of the far bookshelf-covered wall, because I do my best ranting while pacing.

"You don't get to be the only one making the rules here. I have stipulations. No one can know. My family. My employees. *No one.* I don't *ever* want my name linked to yours."

I don't pause to consider the intelligence of what I'm saying, because I'm too pissed to hold back the rest. Furious, I spin and walk in the other direction, keeping my gaze on anything but Lachlan Mount, at least until I've finished making my demands.

"We decide on a mutual time and place to meet. No more of this driver and being collected and hooded. I refuse. You won't leave marks. You won't hurt me. And you sure as hell aren't going to make me disappear when this is all over, because I swear my family and friends will never let you get away with it."

I spin on my stiletto to see just how angry my speech made him . . . and find myself standing in an empty room.

He's gone.

The bastard left? Just like that. Not one fucking word from him?

That motherfucker. I clench my teeth so hard, my jaw aches.

In my anger, I bolt toward the torn paper on the

floor and snatch it up. Holding the two pieces together, I read the words beneath the large, bolded title.

Keira Kilgore will never sign the rights to her company over to Lachlan Mount because she is stubborn, bullheaded, and entirely too loyal to the concept of family tradition. And what's more, he doesn't need her business establishment because he will own her.

That lying piece of shit.

He didn't offer me a real way out.

Or he knows me well enough to realize it would never be a viable option. That possibility might be even scarier. I contemplate the deal I've made with the devil.

What choice do I have? How can I face my father and tell him I lost the company his father and his father's father before him built with blood, sweat, and sacrifice?

My body in exchange for my pride. That's the deal I've struck.

I hate Lachlan Mount.

Even his name sends bolts of heat through me, spawned from wrath unlike anything I've ever experienced.

I hate how he makes me feel.

I hate that my body responds to him.

As the fireplace spins again and Scar returns with the black hood, the voice in my head whispers one more truth.

I hate that I want him to touch me again.

ELEVEN

Mount

I DON'T NEED TO PICTURE THE RAGE ON HER FACE when she reads the bullshit legal document I had prepared for our meeting. It's evident on the monitor on my desk as she crushes it in her clenched fists.

Keira Kilgore was an easy mark. Full of righteous indignation and a fire I'll enjoy having beneath me.

It amuses me that she thought she could make demands. Grown men with brass balls the size of boulders wouldn't dare. That's why she's a fascination. An oddity.

That's all she is.

Entertainment. A piece of property to amuse me for a short time.

I want her willing. I refuse to let it be any other way.

Even defiant and angry, she responded to me like an instrument to a savant. I'll tame that fire. Bend her to my will.

My dick hardens for what seems like the dozenth

time tonight as I picture her submitting to my every command.

That ass.

Those tits.

That tight little cunt.

Property of no man? Bullshit.

Keira Kilgore is *mine*.

TWELVE

Keira

S CAR DOESN'T SPEAK AS HE SLIPS THE HOOD OVER my head and picks me up again. Up, down, around and around.

Is it a spiral staircase?

I feel the cool breeze of outside air for only a moment before he settles me in the backseat of the car. Immediately, my hands go to the hood, but his thick fingers grab them and squeeze. It's a clear indication that I'm not to remove it.

"I have to leave it on for the ride home? Are you joking?"

The only response he gives is a grunt.

My fingers itch to rip the hood off, but if keeping it on gets me home faster, then I'll leave the damn thing alone.

He backs out of the garage, and the muted street noises barely breach the interior of the luxury car. Again, I lose track of which way we turn and instead stay silent, ready for this nightmare of an evening to be over. When the car finally stops again, I sit on my hands, expecting him to take the hood off, but he doesn't.

"Someone is going to see and think you're—"

Grunt.

I shut up and let him lift me out of the car and carry me up to my apartment.

Except something feels off. Keys jingle, but I swear they sound different from mine.

Scar hauls me up the stairs and stands me on my feet while he unlocks dead bolts. He gives me a small shove into the room, and the door shuts behind me before I can yank off the hood.

I rip it over my head and spin around, my brain racing to process something that makes absolutely no sense at all.

This isn't my apartment.

Where the hell am I?

Mount. He did this.

He never intended to let me go.

"Where are you, you fucking bastard?"

I jerk my head from side to side, taking in the walls papered in a sophisticated black-and-white brocade pattern, looking for the telltale globe in the corners of the thick crown molding that would give away the presence of a camera.

I don't see any evidence of a camera, but that doesn't mean there's not one here. But Mount's not here either.

That's something.

Barely.

All the relief I felt on my ride "home" drains from me as I investigate my new cage. I heard the locks. I know I'm not leaving until he lets me. My body trembles, and it has nothing to do with the fact that I'm naked under my coat.

I wrap my arms around myself and chafe them in an attempt to stop the shaking.

Don't think about it. Gather information. Be a general, not a prisoner.

I swallow the fear and focus on my surroundings. There must be something that will help me either figure out where I am or aid me in my escape. I turn, surveying what is probably the most beautiful sitting room I've ever seen. The phrase *gilded cage* has never been so fitting.

There are only three colors in the whole room. Black, white, and gold.

A shiny black door leads off to the right and I rush toward it, hoping like an idiot that it could possibly be an exit, but knowing it won't be at the same time.

It's a bedroom.

Not the overblown bordello of a room I expected before, but one that's sophisticated and feminine. Again, there are only three colors in the decor—black, white, and gold.

The black four-poster bed dominates the room, taking up an entire third, with sheer white fabric leading from post to post. The spread matches the black-and-white brocade from the sitting room walls, and the black satin sheets are already pulled back as if nightly turndown service has already been performed.

He never planned to let me leave. Ever.

The whole production in the library was exactly what Magnolia warned me about—Mount's ability to fuck with my head.

I push the fear away. It's a useless waste of energy.

Another door leads off the bedroom to a luxurious bathroom nicer than in any hotel room I've seen, again done in black, white, and gold.

What is it with these colors?

The bathroom has another door that leads to a walk-in closet that could serve as a decent-sized bedroom itself, but the bars are completely empty. I check the drawers in the center island, and they're empty too.

Does he expect to keep me here naked? At least I have my trusty trench coat.

I think about the dress I was supposed to wear tonight, and for the first time, I wish I'd worn it. I leave the closet behind to inspect the contents of the bathroom drawers. Instead of being bare, they're filled with expensive toiletries of every kind.

I make my way back through the series of rooms to the sitting area and stare at the locked door. Two dead bolts, but instead of knobs to turn on the inside, there are keyholes without the accompanying keys.

Even though I know it's pointless because I heard the bolts slide home, I walk over to it and test the handle.

It pisses me off all over again, though.

"You asshole! You can't keep me like a fucking pet!" I kick at the door with the delicate stilettos and succeed in leaving a tiny mark and stubbing my toe.

After limping to the center of the room, I spin in a circle with my arms outstretched. I can feel, down to the very marrow of my bones, that he is watching me from somewhere.

"Is this what you wanted? A pet? If I don't show up for work tomorrow, everyone will notice. They'll call the police. I don't care how many cops you have on your payroll, there has to be someone you don't own. *They'll find me and you'll pay!* You wanted me willing? Well, fuck you, Mount! This wasn't part of the deal!"

My next instinct is to return to the door and beat on it until my fists are bruised and bloodied and my voice is raw from screaming for someone to let me out.

But I don't. I refuse to give him the satisfaction of seeing me break down. I'm stronger than this. Mount will not win. I harness the anger instead.

In a loud, clear voice, I tell the empty room, "You might get my body willingly, but that's all you'll ever get from me. I swear I will hate you through every single moment of this."

After my speech, my brain slows, exhausted from the events of the last week, and all I want to do is slide between the decadent sheets and go to sleep. But something about that feels like I'm letting him win, and that's one thing I won't do without putting up a fight.

I faced the devil in his lair and came out unscathed. That's something, right? A small victory.

Or mostly unscathed. My still-hard nipples and the heat between my legs remind me all too vividly of the fire he stoked within me.

"Lie to yourself all you want, Keira. But tell me the truth about one thing. When was the last time you were fucked by a real man? Someone who knows what you need. Someone who'll take control from you and give you what you've been dying for. How many times did you have to fuck yourself with your fingers after your limp-dick husband rolled over, just so you would get to come too?"

He's fucking with my head. That's all. He can't know how right he is.

My eyes go to the bed as his final warning replays in my mind.

"Your orgasms belong to me. If you ever touch yourself without my permission, I will spank that pussy of yours until you're begging to come."

With the same defiance that carried me into a henna shop, and then on these extravagantly expensive stilettos into the presence of the most feared man in this city tonight, I make a decision. I may be almost out of ammunition, but I can still fire a parting shot. I stroll into the bedroom and unbelt my trench coat, dropping it on the bedroom floor.

I rip back the spread and study the black sheets. Black like the soul of the man who put me here. I sit and remove each of the exquisite heels and drop them carelessly on the floor before sliding to the center of the bed and spreading my legs.

"This pussy doesn't belong to you yet, Mount."

I reach between my legs, hating that I'm already wet, but grateful at the same time because this won't take long at all.

Am I daring the devil to come bolting through the door to make good on his threat?

No. I'm calling his bluff.

When I come tonight, it'll be a *fuck you* to the man who thinks he owns me. I'll even make sure to use my middle finger.

THIRTEEN

Keira

WHEN I WAKE, IT'S NOT BECAUSE OF SUNLIGHT cutting through the cheap plastic blinds of my bedroom, but a nightmare that jerks me out of a dead sleep.

The room is pitch black, but my heart hammers as I reach for the bedside lamp. Instead of the rickety wooden nightstand I got at Ikea, my fingers graze cool marble.

Oh. Shit.

It wasn't a nightmare.

Finally, I find a switch, and a soft glow fills the black, white, and gold bedroom.

There's no clock. I have no sense of whether it's night or day because there are no windows. Only a locked door to which I have no key.

And no freaking clothes except for my trench coat. Smart, Keira. Really freaking smart. I don't even have my purse. Scar must have left it in the car.

I yank the sheet from the bed and wrap it around my body before heading into the bathroom. I glance at the mirror, wincing at my appearance. My eyeliner is smeared beneath my eyes in dark circles, and my hair is as much of a rat's nest as one would expect, given the way I tossed and turned in the throes of the nightmare.

Except it wasn't a nightmare. It's my new reality.

I leave the expensive products untouched, wanting nothing from Mount except my freedom. That's still all I want, and I'll find a way to get it. Today.

When I turn in the direction of the bedroom, something else catches my eye. A black silk robe hanging on a hook near the glass shower enclosure. It wasn't there last night.

Someone came in while I slept.

The realization hits me with stunning and skin-crawling clarity.

I rush back through the bedroom and out into the sitting area, and sure enough, there are silver-covered dishes on a table with a note.

Eat.

Shower.

Ready yourself in accordance with the instructions on the bedside table if you want to leave these rooms today.

The heavy scrawl is familiar and carries no signature.

What instructions?

I turn back to the bedroom and check the table with the lamp I turned on. It's bare.

The other nightstand, however, is not. There's a black lacquered box.

How the hell did I miss that?

My throat goes bone dry as I swallow and step closer to the box, almost as afraid to lift the lid as I was the last one. But the note said *if you want to leave these rooms today*, and God knows I do.

I open it and stare down at the contents. It's a black and gold . . . sex toy? It looks like a vibrator, but there's a looped cord attached at the gold end, and it doesn't take a genius to figure out what that's for. And yet Mount was thorough enough to leave a note for me anyway.

This will fill your pussy until I let you take my cock.

Let me?

Let me?

If I were capable of breathing fire, I'd burn this entire building down right now.

I read the rest as soon as the red haze clears from my vision.

The clothes you will wear to work are in the closet. If you are not attired as I've outlined by nine, expect to spend another twenty-four hours here. Your excuses will be made to your employees.

The hurricane of emotions rioting through my head has my fingers gripping the device before I'm conscious of my own movement. More than anything, I want to throw it at the wall, smashing it to pieces.

How dare he?

But one phrase stops me before my high-school softball-pitching skills come into play.

"The clothes you will wear to work."

My chest heaves with ragged breaths as I drop onto the edge of the bed and reread every word of the note six times. I don't trust this man, but if there's a single chance he'll let me out of these rooms to go to work, I have to comply.

And he knows I will.

"You fucking bastard," I tell the wall, the pliant latex of the sex toy clutched in my hand.

Mount's low, deep voice comes from the doorway. "You're right. I am a bastard. Born on the streets to a whore who left me on the front steps of a church. Raised on those same streets and put through a hell you will never in your soft and cushioned life ever imagine."

I whip around to face him, my hand no longer shaking in rage, but trembling with fear. He steps toward me, and the stories Magnolia told me play through my head, as do her warnings.

I straighten my arm down at my side, hiding my reaction from him.

"You think what I want from you is demeaning?" he asks, taking another step toward me.

"You don't fucking know the meaning of the word, but I'm happy to introduce you to a taste if that's what it takes for you to hold up your end of the bargain we made last night. Unlike you, I keep my word."

In that moment, I believe he's capable of every horrible thing I've heard about him.

He can hurt me. Kill me. Make me disappear.

But for some reason that I may never, ever understand—he wants me.

That, and maybe only that, gives me an edge.

I have a choice to make, and I can't let fear paralyze my brain. I can continue to rebel and challenge him—and undoubtedly lose—or bend the slightest bit and make it appear that I'm playing his game.

I may be stubborn, but I'm not stupid.

I straighten my shoulders and lift my chin as though the black satin sheet is a ball gown.

"I was not aware of your parentage. The slur was only meant in reference to your personality. At least, what I've seen of it so far." The next part is harder to get out, but I manage. "I apologize for any offense I've caused with it. It was unintended in that context."

Something flits across his expression. *Surprise? Disbelief? Shock?* I don't know, because it's gone as quickly as it came, and he glances down at his watch.

"You have eleven minutes to get ready if you want to go to work today." His gaze lifts to mine and a hint of a smirk tugs at the edge of his mouth. "I suggest you hurry, unless you'd prefer to spend the day wearing less than you are now."

Again, the phrase *fucking bastard* floats through my head, but this time I keep it in. I spin and rush into the bathroom, slamming the door behind me, not even thinking until I'm midway through brushing my teeth that maybe slamming a door in Mount's face might not be the best idea I've ever had.

Even so, I scrub my face in a hurry and rush to the

closet to find exactly one outfit hanging in it. A black pencil skirt and an iridescent gold blouse that looks nearly transparent. A matching sheer gold bra lies on the center island next to a strand of white pearls.

Black, gold, and white.

I don't have time to wonder again about the significance of those colors as I drop the sheet and get dressed. I'm not the least bit surprised when everything fits perfectly. The clothes are all higher quality than I've even allowed myself to dream of owning, and my employees are certainly going to have questions.

But I'm getting out. I get to go to work. I focus on that because it's the only thing that matters right now.

Then I remember the black-and-gold device I left on the bathroom counter as I leave the closet.

I don't need instructions to know where it goes, or the significance of the fact that I wasn't provided any panties.

The door to the bathroom opens without invitation.

"Three minutes, Ms. Kilgore." His gaze darts to the item I've just been contemplating. Again, one corner of his mouth tugs up. "I see you're not finished preparing yourself."

Our gazes clash and I stand straight, my chin lifted with pride as our battle of wills plays out in silence. We both know I'm going to lose.

"Are you going to do the honors, or am I?" he asks.

The question sends a bolt of heat straight to my core, even though the opposite should be true. I wish that dark stare turned me ice cold, but it does nothing but spark a firestorm.

"I was just getting to that. If you'll please excuse me for another moment."

My request is overly polite, and apparently amuses him because both corners of Mount's lips tug upward. Instead of leaving, he leans one broad shoulder against the doorway.

"You're forgetting who gives the orders here. Pull up your skirt, bend over, and fill your pussy with that toy or I'll gladly do it myself." He pauses, his grin turning wicked. "Actually, fuck that. If you don't do it right now, the next thing filling your cunt will be my cock as I fuck you across that countertop and watch you come in the mirror."

Sweet Jesus. I cover my mouth with both hands to silence the shocked breath I suck in. The filthy words that fall from his lips go straight to my core as wetness gathers, already threatening to drip down my thighs.

I reach for the toy with one hand and pull the front of my skirt up as discreetly as possible with the other, keeping my bare ass pointing in the direction of the closet and away from his view.

I should have known better.

He shakes his head. "Face the mirror. Bend over."

The fear that filled me last night when he told me to bend over is absent this morning, and in its place is the rage I harnessed. But something else burns just as brightly. It's like he's tapped into a need I didn't know existed. Like I actually *want* someone to tell me to do these dirty things to myself.

I force that thought from my mind as I follow his command, bringing the toy to my entrance.

"I'm willing to bet you don't even need lube."

I squeeze my eyes shut because he's not wrong. The latex of the toy slides against my slickness.

"Fuck yourself with it first."

I heave in a breath and do as he says, pushing the toy in and pulling it out, teasing myself almost to the brink. I shove it in harder, needing only the tiniest bit of stimulation on my clit to push me over the edge. My other hand sneaks around, but he growls another command.

"Stop."

With the toy fully seated inside me, I freeze.

What the hell am I doing? About to get myself off in front of a man I hate?

I stand straight, almost quickly enough to lose my balance, and smooth the skirt down. When I turn to face him, I pretend none of this ever happened.

At least, until one hand disappears into his pocket and the toy comes to life, vibrating inside me.

My knees go weak at the shock, and I fumble for the edge of the countertop to stay upright.

"Oh my God . . ." It's a breathy whisper, and I hope to hell he can't hear it.

I'm not that lucky.

He stalks toward me, meeting my gaze. "That's not what you said last night when you made yourself come."

The punishment he promised me flashes through my brain, and he must read it in my expression. My orgasm is just within reach . . . and the vibrations stop.

"I don't have time to deal with your naughty little

cunt and fingers this morning, but I will. In my world, no one gets away with breaking my rules. I have a feeling you'll learn quickly."

My fingertips clutch the edge of the counter to keep myself from slapping the smug look off his face. Instead, I stand silently in front of him. Apparently, Mount doesn't need or want words from me.

"Get out of my sight while I'm still inclined to let you. Other than using the bathroom, don't you dare take it out without my approval. I promise you won't enjoy the punishment if you do."

I suck in a breath and bolt for the door to the bedroom. I round the side of the bed, grab the stilettos from last night and my trench coat, and practically run for the sitting room door that's cracked open the barest inch.

Outside, Scar is waiting. Hood in hand.

I hate that fucking hood.

But right now, I hate Mount even more.

I rip the hood from Scar's hand and put it over my head myself, and let him carry my rigid body out of my gilded cage.

FOURTEEN

Keira

A S SOON AS WE PULL IN THE PARKING LOT ACROSS the street from the distillery, Scar grunts for me to remove the hood. I ask him to wait and rummage through my purse, which thankfully was still in the car from last night. Surprisingly, he complies while I pull out my emergency makeup stash and bring some semblance of normalcy to my face.

The stilettos I have on from last night are fuck-me shoes of the finest—the most expensive shoes I've ever worn—and there is no way any of this outfit will go unnoticed. The fitted gold shirt hugs my curves and tucks into the pencil skirt that emphasizes my hips and ass way more than I'm comfortable with. The white string of pearls lies against my throat like a collar.

I will fucking kill him if he ever tries to put a leash on me.

I snap my compact closed once I determine I'm as good as I'm going to get, and too pissed off to do any better of a job on my makeup.

Plus, there's the distraction of the high-tech version of Ben Wa balls inside me, and the knowledge that Mount holds the remote has my thighs practically slipping together from my body's response.

The two warring parts of my brain can't reconcile what's happening to me.

How can I hate the man so much, and yet my body loves what he's doing to it?

It's a mystery I won't solve in this parking lot. I reach for the door handle, but Scar stops me with a grunt and hands a note back to me.

If you tell anyone anything, you'll be attending their funeral.

I crumple the note and toss it between the front seats. "Tell him his twisted secret is safe. For today, anyway."

As soon as I utter the last word and shove open the door, the toy inside me buzzes to life for a single instant, like a shock to correct an animal's behavior. I jerk around, looking to see where he is. He has to be close, right? What is the distance on this thing?

Knowing Mount and the power he wields, it's probably miles.

I fucking hate him.

I force myself to slide out of the car, my head held high and my shoulders straight, and walk across the street like absolutely nothing is out of the ordinary.

Certainly not like I've sold my body and my

freedom to save my family's legacy.

I nod at employees, smiling and greeting them like usual, hoping like hell they don't notice anything different about me. The London Fog trench coat is something they've seen before. It's what's under it that will raise eyebrows.

As soon as I enter my office, Temperance pops out of the seat across from my desk, and my heart bangs against my ribs.

"Thank God! I was about to send a search party out after you. You haven't answered any of my texts this morning. The head of operations for the Voodoo Kings wants to meet over lunch to discuss the valet proposition I laid out, and he made it very clear that he wanted you there because, apparently, he doesn't think I have the authority to make any decisions. Which I guess I don't. But still, he was an asshole about it."

When my pulse calms down to nearly healthy levels, I lie through my teeth. "Sorry, I . . . had car trouble this morning. Had to get an Uber. The first one didn't show, and I must've forgot to turn my notifications back on. I . . . turned them off last night to brainstorm some ideas."

Temperance studies me, not exactly like an alien has entered the office, but with enough curiosity that I wonder how I'm going to be able to keep up this charade.

"That's actually smart. Sometimes, all you need is a little quiet time alone for your brain to unleash its full potential. I've heard meditation is incredible. Obviously, we both know that I don't have the patience for that kind of thing, but I bet it would be awesome for your stress. Maybe you should download an app or something."

The quiet time alone I had last night was spent contemplating how to escape a locked room, or alternatively, kill a man without putting everyone I know and love at risk. Not exactly the meditation Temperance is talking about.

"Okay, well, I'm here now, so brief me on what I need to know." I reach for the belt of my coat and untie it before tossing it over the antique coatrack in the corner.

"Holy shit. You look . . . *damn.*"

Fuck. I knew this would happen.

I try to shrug off her response. "I'm trying one of those new subscription boxes. This was what they sent me. It's not like I have the time or inclination to shop anyway, right?" The ease with which more lies fall from my lips should probably concern me, but I comfort myself with one thought—it's in Temperance's best interest never to know that men like Mount exist. Especially him, specifically.

"Well, it looks more like one of those *rent the runway* type things. You're going to have to tell me exactly where you got it, because you look smokin' hot." She pinches her lips shut. "Sorry, you're my boss, so I probably shouldn't say that, right?"

I shake my head. "It's fine. Just . . . trying something new."

"Well, I'd say it's working for you. You're going to knock those guys *dead* at lunch. They'll be so busy checking you out, they'll probably agree to anything we say. I'll make sure to have the contracts ready to sign."

She sits in the seat across from my desk again and fills me in on all the details so I'm prepped for the meeting, but I have trouble concentrating because of the *thing* inside me.

He won't turn it on while I'm at work, right?

I find myself asking the question over and over while Temperance runs down the list of bullet points we need to emphasize during the meeting, and I'm nodding like I agree with everything she's saying but I'm not hearing a word.

There's only one thing on my mind, and it's him.

Magnolia warned me he'd fuck with my head, and he's doing that royally. I have to pull myself back. Find my center. I have to get back to business and pretend I've never heard his name.

"Right, so since we didn't even get to discuss the price changes on the menu upgrade yet, that's on the table to negotiate today. I think we should have Odile prepare and serve both options for lunch, and they can taste the difference. The food will sell itself."

I finally get a grip on the conversation. "But we don't stock what they requested for our normal menu."

Temperance smiles with a wink. "I called in a favor from the meat supplier, and they're bringing it over within the hour."

I lean back in my chair. *The same chair Mount sat in.*

Stop it, Keira.

"How did you get him to agree to that? He's an

asshole about changing delivery days."

Temperance's gaze drifts up to the ceiling. "Well
. . . I had to agree to have drinks with him tomorrow
night, but I plan on coming down with a massive case
of something very contagious. Like, you know, herpes."

I'm thankful I'm not sipping my normal morning
coffee, because I'd spit it out all over the desk.

"Please tell me you're joking."

"Nope. I figure that will end his constant badger-
ing. Who wants to deal with that for the rest of their
life? I mean, ewww." Temperance rubs her nose. "But,
crap, what if it gets back to my mom? They go to the
same church. God, I can just hear the lecture now. 'I
didn't raise no whore, Temperance Jane.'" The last sentence comes out in a perfectly pitched bayou accent,
and I force out a laugh.

*My mama didn't raise a whore either, but that's ex-
actly what I am now*, I think as my inner muscles clench
around the toy.

*How can I hate him and still let him turn me on like
this?* Maybe it's not him. Maybe it's the fact that my
husband didn't touch me for weeks before he died.

I can grieve and hate at the same time, so why can't
I desire and hate at the same time?

"So, now the only issue we have left is getting Odile
to agree," Temperance says with a syrupy-sweet smile.

"And you want me to do it." It's not a question. I
already know the answer.

"You're the boss, boss." Temperance gathers her paperwork and stands. "She keeps telling you to act more
like a CEO, so I figured now is the perfect time to grant

her wish."

I open my mouth to respond, but a sharp buzz rips through the toy for a single blazing moment. My harsh indrawn breath takes us both by surprise.

Temperance hugs the documents to her chest. "If it's that much of an issue, I can—"

I force a smile on my face and squeeze my thighs shut. "Of course not. I—it will be fine. I'll take care of Odile. You draft up the fancy presentations and make it look as expensive as we're going to be."

"We got this, boss. They're not going to walk away now. I've heard the GM has a fondness for Seven Sinners, especially the Spirit of New Orleans blend, so don't be surprised if you get requests the night of the event to put a case or six aside for him."

Temperance refers to our most exclusive whiskey that isn't even available for purchase yet, except by the glass in our restaurant. I took a risk and had sample bottles made and sent to every heavy hitter in town as a gift. I made the decision in the fog of grief and out of desperation with one look at how badly our financial position was after Brett's skimming of the accounts. The gesture was too expensive, and so far hasn't yielded much in return. But maybe this is fate. Everything happens for a reason, right?

Like the vibrator between my legs being controlled by the most dangerous man I've ever met?

Suddenly my closely held belief in pre-destiny and fate and all that goes along with it is called into question.

Everyone comes into your life for a reason . . . or

that's what I always thought. I can't come up with a reason for Mount. I'm sure no one can.

Temperance pauses at the door. "I'll let you figure out how you're going to work on Odile. I'll be in my office running copies and binding presentations if you need me."

I manage the barest of nods as Temperance scoots out of my office, already worrying about the next thing on her to-do list.

That was me just over a week ago. Hell, that was me since the day I took the reins as CEO. All business. It turned out to be my saving grace, and the only way I could cope with the betrayal and fallout from Brett's death.

Hate.

Anger.

Rage.

How sad is it that those emotions are taking up more room in my heart than anything positive in these last months?

What is happening to me?

A con artist with an expensive drug habit and a mistress.

A man who thinks the rules don't apply to him.

As my thighs clench again involuntarily, I swear to myself.

He will not break me.

FIFTEEN

Keira

'M SEATED AT THE TABLE ACROSS FROM THE VOODOO Kings' assistant general manager, the public relations director, and the special event coordinator of the football team when Carlie, one of my waitresses, brings out the first flight of whiskey.

If anyone thinks I'm above getting these men drunk, they'd be wrong. They have the power to sign the contract that will help haul my company's ass out of hot water, and that means I have no choice but to get this contract signed.

Am I proud of it? Not particularly. Am I willing to do it anyway? Absolutely. Am I also thanking the good Lord above that not a single one of the people sitting across the table from me is female and would likely see right through my ploy? Damn right.

"Gentlemen, let's start this meeting off properly— with a damned good whiskey made in our hometown in the Irish tradition of my family." I reach for a glass and lift it toward the center of the table.

They each grab their own glass. None of them seem to notice Temperance doesn't. While I've been sipping on whiskey like mother's milk for almost thirty years, she barely drinks at all. I tease her about being a cheap date.

Each man raises a glass, and we clink the rims together.

"Sláinte," I say as a burst of vibration unleashes between my legs, and I nearly drop my drink.

The men tip back their whiskey, not noticing that I'm struggling to lift mine to my lips because of the waves of pleasure tearing through me.

I chug the drink, needing it now more than ever, and shift in my chair, praying this is going to stop as quickly as the last one.

The assistant GM leans forward, his eyes not on mine, but on the deep V cut of my blouse.

"So, Keira. I understand you've been doing a bang-up job with the distillery since you took the helm from your dad."

I'm too distracted by the vibrations between my legs to decide if he's giving me a compliment or mocking me.

"The last few months have been a little trying, but like my ancestors, I push forward." I have no idea where that response comes from, and force my lips to curve into a smile as an orgasm builds in my core. "Tenacity and the Irish go hand in . . . hand." I struggle to get the last word out.

I'm in serious danger of coming when the

vibrations suddenly stop. I don't know if I want to kill the man with the remote or kiss him for not making me embarrass myself in public.

Kiss him? Are you freaking insane, Keira?

The pleasure recedes as quickly as it started.

Never. I'll be like freaking Julia Roberts before she stupidly fell for Richard Gere in Pretty Woman. *No kissing on the mouth. Ever. I'm making it a rule.*

"Tenacious, indeed. Must go along with that red hair of yours. Do you have the temper to match?"

Again, the assistant GM's eyes are on my cleavage, and I can't help but look down in response.

Oh. Fuck.

My nipples, in the sheer bra Mount picked, are on high beams. They clearly haven't gotten the memo that there's no longer an orgasm coming.

I return my glass to the table harder than necessary, and the thwack of glass against metal causes his eyes to jerk up to my face.

"I don't have a temper. That's a redhead myth." I smile as I lie, something I'm entirely too good at today for comfort. "Now, let's discuss the amazing package we've put together for you."

Thankfully, Temperance takes this as her cue to jump in. "As you've requested and we briefly discussed, we've come up with a perfect solution to any PR issues with our valet parking—"

"I still think you're insane if you think these guys will take it well when you won't hand their keys back at the end of the night," the PR director says, interrupting her.

The event coordinator looks at him. "You deal with the bullshit these assholes pull more than anyone, and I agree with you."

All three men look across the table, their gazes shifting between Temperance and me, and she takes the lead. "We'll spin it as a complimentary black-car service. They can have as much fun as they want. Indulge and then be delivered home without a single worry."

The GM huffs. "Maybe if you put a hooker in each car, then you'd tempt some of them."

The vibrator springs to life again, but this time only for an instant. Long enough for my nipples to have zero hope of disappearing from view through my blouse.

I grip the edge of the table, and words I never intended to say spring from my lips. "If that's what it takes . . ."

All three men zero in on my face. A smug smile drifts over the assistant GM's lips, and the toy comes to life again.

I'm going to kill Mount.

"You are a sassy redhead. I like it. The team, of course, couldn't condone such a practice or pay for it, but damned if it wouldn't be a hell of an idea."

The vibrations don't quit, which means I have to brazen this out. "I'm joking, gentlemen. Of course, we couldn't have anything to do with something like that. We might be in the business of sin, but not that kind."

Carlie chooses that perfect moment to serve the appetizers, and another server, Dena, holds the second flight of whiskey.

I have no idea how I manage to speak, but my voice rises to a higher octave, and I pretend it's from the excitement of the food. "Oh, perfect! Thank you, ladies!"

Temperance looks at me strangely, no doubt noticing that I have one hand fisted on my skirt as I fight the waves of desire driving through me.

I'm going to kill him, I think again.

Temperance takes over the conversation, explaining what the appetizers are and that they're in line with the original budget. I squeeze my eyes closed as the men gorge on the food.

My assistant leans over and whispers in my ear. "Are you okay? Seriously, you're acting weird."

"Migraine. Just hit me. I'm powering through."

Her face morphs into an expression of sympathy. "Do you need to go?"

Yes, I want to scream, but the vibrator stops.

"No. I'm fine. Not a problem."

None of the men notice anything beyond the incredible food and even better whiskey we ply them with for the next hour.

By the time we finish, the signed contract is on the table, including the upcharge for the black-car service and the food.

I rise from my seat and step out from behind the table, and they follow suit.

"It's going to be a fabulous event, gentlemen. You won't regret your choice, and with an open bar featuring not only our incredible whiskey but every other brand of top-shelf liquor, your fundraiser is going to be a massive success."

"I couldn't agree more." The assistant GM reaches out to shake my hand, and again, his eye contact is lacking.

As soon as our palms meet, the vibrator comes to life, and I squeeze his hand and drop it just as quickly. I get the same buzz, almost like a warning with each handshake.

Oh, you motherfucker. Where are you? The question burns in my brain, but I keep my businesslike smile pasted on my face as Temperance leads them to the elevator.

"I need to speak with Odile, so I'll be down in a few. Have a wonderful day, gentlemen."

As soon as the metal doors slide shut, I spin around on my stilettos from last night and survey the restaurant. We had a small lunch crowd, but the man at the top of my list of *people who need killing* is absent.

Would he have given the remote to one of his employees to control? The thought repulses me, spawning another disgusting thought. *Am I just a toy to be handed off and played with by anyone? Is he really set on making me a whore?*

I scan the restaurant, and some of the people meet my gaze and smile politely, but there's no one who stands out with a flashing red beacon that says *I work for Lachlan Mount and I'm fucking with your life.*

I wait for the elevator to return to the top floor, eager to get back to my basement where I can—

What? What can I do? I have no power here.

"Don't let him walk all over you." That was

Magnolia's advice.

Not letting him walk all over me would mean stepping into the ladies' room and taking this *thing* out of me right now and throwing it in the trash.

"Don't you dare take it out without my approval. I promise you won't enjoy the punishment if you do." Mount's warning is burned into my brain.

I don't even want to think about what punishment he'd come up with, but then again, I can't let him call all the shots.

It's one thing for him to mess with my head while I'm in his territory, but it's something completely different when I'm trying to do business. It was one of my stipulations—one he obviously didn't care about hearing because he disappeared.

Screw him and his punishments. Bring it on, Mount.

I turn to head for the ladies' room, but another vibration buzzes against my leg.

It's not the toy this time. It's my phone.

As I release a long breath, I reach into the pocket of the pencil skirt and pull it out, half expecting to see Mount's name on the screen. But it's not, thankfully, and seeing a picture of my mom's smiling face on my phone helps bring me back to center and remind me why I'm doing this.

I answer with the first genuine smile I've had in days, and duck into a corner alcove of the hall that leads to the guest restrooms. "Hey, Mom, how are you? How's Dad?"

"We're good! Great, really. My golf game has improved immeasurably, but that's not important. I'm calling to see how you're holding up."

Her mention of golf reminds me of the picture I was given as a warning.

"I'm fine. Everything's great." I hope my tone is convincing, but when she replies, I know it's not.

"Sweetie . . . have you reached out to that counselor yet? I really think you need to talk to someone about all of this. Burying those conflicting feelings about Brett's death isn't coping. You need to talk it out. Express your anger."

I think of all the rage I've felt since Mount appeared in my office.

My mom continues. "And your grief too. Even though you were going to divorce him, that's like a death in itself."

"I'm fine, Mom. Really. I am. If it makes you feel better, I'll join a kickboxing class to express my anger."

As soon as the words come out, I remember that I no longer have control of those kinds of decisions in my life. I'll be picked up and returned to my cell at the end of the day.

"Sweetheart, it's not the same. It doesn't make you weak to ask for help."

If she only knew how much help I need right now . . . *But she can never know.*

"Look, we both know that this conversation is going to end with me telling you that the best therapy for me is burying myself in work and fixing all the things Brett screwed up before he . . . passed." I fumble on the last word because it's still hard to talk about. I was so angry, but at one time, I thought I loved him, and thinking of the horrific way he died . . . I wouldn't wish that on anyone.

The long-suffering sigh that I swear all mothers have perfected comes through my phone. "Lord knows I want to argue with you, but your father would say the same thing."

"How is Dad?"

Part of the reason my dad finally relinquished control of the company to me was because his doctor warned him that he was a perfect case of someone waiting until sixty-five to retire, only to die at sixty-six because he overworked himself for years. My mother wouldn't allow such a thing, so she forced him to retire. I want to think he would have gotten there eventually on his own, but knowing my father, it's highly doubtful.

"He's doing great. The most stressful thing in his life is his golf handicap, and his last physical came back with better numbers than we've seen in years." The relief is clear in my mom's tone.

"And probably whether or not he gets his payment from me every month," I can't help but add.

"Keira, stop. He knows you're more passionate about that old distillery than either of your sisters, and would die before you'd let it fail. He believes in you, even if he doesn't say it often enough. We're both so proud of you."

She doesn't realize how badly I need to hear those words right now. Then again, how proud would my parents be if they knew I've whored myself out to keep the legacy alive?

Shame slithers through my soul for what I'm doing.

I have no choice.

But that doesn't mean I have to like it.

"Thank you, Mom. I love you both. I'm glad Dad's finally learning to chill out."

"Oh, honey. I didn't say that. He's already president of the condo association and trying to institute some kind of rules about the golf carts. The man is incapable of being anything but exactly what he is—a CEO. But that's why I love him. His drive. His fire. He had me from day one. No doubt about it."

Knowing that she's about to launch into the story of their first date for quite possibly the six hundredth time in my life, I interject. "I know, and someday I hope I find out what that's like."

I don't really mean it, though. Brett's death and betrayal are still too fresh for me to even consider wanting to get married again. Maybe ever. But my parents are proof that sometimes it truly can last.

My mom makes a sound of approval. "You have no idea how happy that makes me. I want nothing more than for you to move forward with your life and find someone who will love you like you were always meant to be loved. That's what I want for all my girls. Someone to treat you all like queens."

Lachlan Mount may be the king of New Orleans' underworld, but he sure as hell will never treat me like a queen. And that's not even an option, so why the hell would I even think such a thing? It's my mother. Her pep talks cause temporary insanity on occasion.

"I have a meeting coming up, so I have to let you go. But I love you, and it's so good to hear your voice. I miss you both," I tell her.

"You know I'll be there on the first flight if you need me, honey. I'm due for a real beignet soon."

The thought of having my mother in the same town as Mount is even more of a nightmare than my life is currently. I couldn't even begin to explain or lie to cover this up.

"We're so busy right now with this big event coming up, and you know if you come, Dad will want to. We both know he'll be right back in the thick of things, stressing out about all the details, and neither of us wants that for him."

My mom sighs. "And he'd be stepping on your toes. I know. I know. But soon. You'll have to come visit us when you can get away for a few days."

Get away has a whole new meaning now that I spent a night in captivity.

"I will. I promise. As soon as I can." To myself, I add silently, *Or as soon as I happen upon an extra half million dollars, because that would solve all my problems.*

"Okay, sweetheart. Talk soon."

"Tell Imogen and Jury I said hi," I add, knowing she's going down the list of daughters to call and check on.

"Absolutely. One of these days, I'll have you all together again for a happy occasion. It's going to happen. One of y'all is gonna have to get married and have babies sometime soon."

"Bye, Mom." I disconnect the call, hating how much of that conversation was made up of lies.

My sisters and I couldn't have less in common, and I haven't seen either of them since Brett's funeral. It actually shocked me they both showed up.

Imogen has buried herself in her dissertation, determined to land an incredible postdoc position that will launch her fantastic career. She's the overachiever of the family, but was truly sympathetic at the funeral, some of the only true emotion I've seen from her in years. She's not a typical middle child. She doesn't act out. She keeps all of her emotions locked down.

Then there's Jury, who gallivants around the globe, shaking her ass on bars for money. She was a total bitch at the funeral. I believe her exact words were, "Couldn't have picked a better end for that bastard myself."

I slapped her across the face and walked away while Imogen gasped and ordered her to have some respect for once in her life.

Jury showed no remorse. Cheaters apparently deserve no sympathy in her book, which makes me wonder who cheated on her in the past, but we don't have that kind of relationship. I know as much about my sisters' lives right now as they do about mine, and for once in my life, I'm thankful for that. This isn't something I want them anywhere near.

I tuck my phone into my pocket and take a step in the direction of the elevator, only for the toy to come to life again.

I shuffle toward the steel doors like a little girl

who's about to pee her pants, and punch the call button with my finger. With a glance skyward, I force myself to think about anything but the buzzing between my legs.

Just stop. Please stop.

Once I'm in the elevator, I watch the numbers as it heads for the basement, desperate to get into my office before I spontaneously combust.

I'm going to come.

There's no ifs, ands, or buts about it.

I shoulder open the office door and burst inside, ready to moan with my release—and the toy shuts off.

My desk lamp is on, and just like he had once before, Mount sprawls in my desk chair like a king on his throne.

"You son of a bitch! Where were you? In the restaurant? Watching my meeting? Trying to screw this up for me? Do you want me to fail? Is that the whole point of this? Because I won't. You can try to fuck with my head all you want, but I won't let you take down my business too."

He leans forward, resting his forearms on my desk. His black-and-diamond cufflinks wink in the desk-lamp light. "Lock the door."

My chest, heaving with all the righteous indignation pent up from my speech, stills immediately. "This is my office. You don't control things here." I'm proud my voice doesn't waver.

Mount spreads his hands and presses both face-down on my desk as he rises halfway out of his chair. "You still don't get it." His tone takes on an amused quality for a moment before it turns sharp. "Don't make me repeat myself, Keira."

When I don't move, he stands to his full height, his hands at his sides. "Lock the fucking door."

The order is delivered with such quiet menace, I have no option but obedience. I reach back without looking behind me and flip the lock. In the muted light, his shadowed expression is unreadable, but I can't imagine it means anything good for me.

"I watched you. I watched them watch you."

"How? You weren't there."

He doesn't answer my question. "They wanted to fuck you. Did you feel it?"

I recall the way the men stared at my chest and my embarrassingly hard nipples. "Only because of what you made me wear."

He steps out from behind my desk. "Wrong. You don't see it. You're totally fucking clueless about what men think when they look at you. Except today. Today, you felt it."

I don't know how to respond, but Mount doesn't need anything from me to continue.

"But none of them can have you because you belong to me. Get over here."

When I don't move, he slips a hand into his pocket and the toy buzzes to life, this time at a new, more intense setting.

My hands clench into fists, and I hold back a whimper as pleasure courses through me. Spending the entire morning being teased and on the verge of coming has me sliding closer and closer to the edge.

"Don't you fucking come." His voice takes on a growling tone with his command.

"I can't stop—" It's there. Almost within my grasp as I clench my thighs together and wait for ecstasy to burst through me.

And then it stops.

"You bastard!"

He closes the distance between us in three strides and clamps a hand around my hip.

"You shouldn't get to fucking come until I do, and you already owe me. How many more debts do you want to rack up?"

I tell myself the light-headedness hitting me is because I'm about to hyperventilate, and not because of him. I barely manage a response. "I don't want to owe you another goddamned thing."

"Too late. Now I just have to decide how you're going to get me off first. Hands, mouth, tits, pussy, or ass."

I try to cover my involuntary thigh clench, but he doesn't miss it. *He doesn't miss anything.*

Mount's nostrils flare, and his gaze burns into me. "I could get you off in less than a minute. One touch to your clit, another pulse of the vibrator, and you'll be moaning my name. I own your orgasms. I decide when you come. Not you. Learn it. Live it. Because you're going to fucking love it by the time I'm done with you."

"Never." I emphasize both syllables of the word, realizing that apparently my new strategy has morphed into me standing my ground or dying while I try. And with Mount, dying might be a very real possibility.

With one swift motion, he has my back pressed against the door, the hand at my hip gripping tighter and the other up my skirt.

I expect him to go straight for my pussy, but all he does is slide a finger up along my inner thighs.

"You're dripping because of *me.*"

His finger finds the loop on the end of the toy and he tugs. The unexpected movement tears a moan from my throat. He pulls it partway out and pushes it back in, fucking me slowly with each stroke.

He's trying to kill me by keeping me on edge. I bite my lip and squeeze my eyes shut.

"Don't be a coward. Open your fucking eyes."

I do, and I meet his black gaze. It's filled with triumph.

"All you have to do is ask for it." It's like the devil offering up your deepest desire for the low, low price of your soul.

"Fuck. You." There's no power behind the words because my body teeters on the edge of detonation.

"No, Keira. I'm fucking you. I'm the *only one* fucking you."

His thumb sweeps across my clit, and I'm done. The orgasm crashes through my body like a hurricane. Uncontrollable. Wild. Untamed.

I try to stifle my moan, but I can't. I come apart, staring into the soulless black eyes of a man I hate, but one who plays my body like he's been given an owner's manual I didn't know existed.

He presses harder against my clit, and I ride the storm for all it's worth. I can't help it. It's too good not to wring every drop I can steal from it.

When he yanks the toy free, I'm not ready. My mouth drops open as he lifts it from beneath my skirt.

My first thought is so jacked up, I don't even want to voice it.

Put it back. I want it back.

He holds the black-and-gold vibrator between us, coated in my slickness, and I'm forced to face my shame.

How can I let him do this to me?

"This should be covering my cock right now. But you have to earn that privilege."

His infuriating words roar through me. *Earn it? He should be so lucky.*

Mount reaches for my hand and closes my fingers around the slippery toy. "This better be in your pussy when you're delivered to me."

He steps back, and I stumble away from the door. With one flip of the lock and a creak of the wood, Mount disappears, and I'm left holding a sex toy and have no idea what the hell just happened.

I legitimately think I could kill him with my bare hands. But I also want him more than I've ever wanted any man in my life.

It's visceral. Primal. Uncontrollable.

Magnolia warned me, but I didn't understand the full magnitude of that warning. Or maybe I didn't understand how badly I need what he gives me.

Everything about this situation is fucked up beyond belief. I want to fight him to my last breath, but at the same time, I want to dig my nails into his back as he pounds into me until I scream in ecstasy.

My hand clenches around the toy, and I quiver at the thought of putting it back in.

Mount claims he owns my orgasms.

I'm starting to believe he's right.

SIXTEEN

Keira

I DON'T KNOW WHY I EVEN BOTHER ATTEMPTING TO
work for the rest of the day. I can't concentrate on
anything except the sex toy that I washed in my
small connected private bathroom, wrapped in a paper
towel, and shoved in my purse—after I spent nearly an
hour removing the henna.

Five o'clock comes and goes, but I don't leave the
office. The longer I stay here, the longer I can put off
following another one of his orders.

It's after seven when someone knocks on my office
door. My shoulders tense immediately, and I squeeze the
edges of my desk.

It's not him, I tell myself as I force my body to relax.
Mount would never knock.

I call out for whoever it is to enter, and Temperance
pokes her head in.

"I thought I saw your light still on. I figured after our
victory today, you'd be out celebrating."

Out celebrating. Something I no longer have the freedom to do . . . or do I?

"You know me, workaholic to the core."

"That's the truth. Which is why I brought the celebration to you." She produces a bottle of champagne from behind her back.

I stare at the bottle in surprise. "I didn't think you drank. You never try the whiskey."

Her teeth catch her bottom lip, and she looks at me with a sheepish expression. "This might get me fired, but . . . I just don't like whiskey."

I pretend to cross myself like I'm a priest and she sinned in my presence. "Are you serious?"

She nods and her smile returns. "I'm sure Seven Sinners is the best there is, which is why I can market the hell out of it. But after this one night, freshman year of college, where my brand-new roommate ended up holding the garbage can while I puked from the top bunk in our dorm room, I haven't been able to touch the stuff again."

I bring my hands together in a steeple, with my index fingers pressing against the bridge of my nose, and picture it with a laugh. "Fair enough. I have a similar aversion to gin. It tastes way too much like those pine-tree air fresheners when you puke it up. Or, at least, the cheap gin I drank in college did. Now I stick to good whiskey."

"Only Seven Sinners?"

I shake my head. "No, I make sure to sample as much of the competition as possible. You have to know what your rivals are doing to make sure you're doing it better."

She lifts the bottle of champagne in her hand. "So, does that mean no champagne toast to celebrate?"

There's so much hopefulness in her voice, coupled with the fact that I'm in absolutely no hurry to leave, I can't help but agree. "I've got some glasses we can use. They're not champagne flutes, but it means we don't have to go upstairs to track some down."

Temperance grins. "I'm not fancy. I was willing to settle for the company coffee mugs." She takes one of the leather club chairs on the opposite side of my desk and holds out the bottle. "Want to do the honors?"

I remember the last time I popped a champagne cork. It was in my townhouse on my wedding night, and Brett couldn't manage to get it open.

Now I wonder if alcohol was all he had that night. Any good memories I tried to hold on to after his betrayal are now tainted by what Magnolia told me. My husband was a con man and a cokehead, as well as a cheating son of a bitch. I force the knowledge down as I accept the bottle from Temperance.

"Absolutely." I grab the tumblers from below the liquor shelf behind my desk, used to showcase Seven Sinners whiskeys throughout the years, and set them on the blotter.

I pop the cork without making a mess and fill them almost to the brim.

"Whoa. A little more heavy-handed with your pouring than normal?" Temperance comments.

Instead of responding, I lift my glass, which prompts her to do the same. "Sláinte."

We clink the crystal together, and I take a healthy

swallow. It's a perfect balance of sweet and dry, and an added bonus—the bubbles go straight to my head as I concentrate on draining the entire thing.

Yes, this is exactly *what I needed after this afternoon.*

I set my glass down and turn the bottle around to investigate the label more thoroughly. I don't recognize the name, but that doesn't mean much. I don't keep up with the wine business.

"Nice choice," I say as I refill my glass. When I look up, Temperance's gaze locks on mine.

"I know the last few months have been rough. If there's anything I can do, more I can take off your plate, just let me know. I'm here to help."

She's sweet, and a hell of an employee, but she has no clue why I would really like to finish this entire bottle myself. *Maybe if I'm drunk when I go back to Mount's* . . . As soon as the thought crosses my mind, I know it's the wrong move. I need my wits about me when I face him, and while I can drink whiskey all day and not have an issue, champagne is a completely different story.

"Or if you ever want to talk about what happened—"

I raise my glass to my lips again, and when I set it down, I drop my hands into my lap. "You've already taken on plenty. Hell, you deserve a raise, and as soon as we get the check from the Voodoo Kings, you'll get one."

Her expression changes into one of excitement. "Really? That would be amazing. The last time I was offered a raise, there was no way I was agreeing to the terms." As soon as the words are out, she looks like she wants to snatch them back.

"What are you talking about? Here?"

Guilt floods her features as she shakes her head vigorously. "No. Uh, another job. Somewhere else."

I study her closer. "You're a terrible liar."

This time it's Temperance lifting her champagne to gulp it down.

"Tell me." I already have a sick feeling twisting in my stomach. Intuition. It's about time I developed some.

"I shouldn't. It doesn't matter anymore."

I lean both elbows on my desk, my glass hanging between my thumbs and forefingers. "Just freaking tell me. Whatever you say stays between us and will have zero impact on your job. I promise." What I tell her is the absolute truth, because there's no way I can afford to lose her.

She refills her glass and takes another sip. "Let's just say that if it hadn't been for you being kind of my idol in the business world, and the shitty state of the job market around here, I would've quit as soon as Brett came on board."

"What did he say to you?"

The color drains from her face and her gaze darts around the room, eager to land anywhere but on me. "I submitted a request for a raise, but I didn't realize you'd already left for a meeting. Brett reviewed it and called me into his office to discuss." She pours another measure of champagne down her throat, as if needing the liquid courage.

I, on the other hand, need it to numb the rage boiling through me. "And?"

"He said that if I wanted a raise, I'd have to earn it the old-fashioned way. I thought he meant working harder." She pauses, her lips pressed together as if not wanting to voice the rest of the horrible truth. I nod, prompting her to continue. "He unzipped his pants and told me I better get to sucking." She chokes on the last part, just like I would choke the life out of Brett if he were still alive.

I reach for the bottle of champagne and refill both our glasses. "I am so fucking sorry. I can't apologize enough. You should've quit. Hell, you should've filed a sexual harassment suit. I would've if I were you."

A moment of silence passes as we both drink.

"I looked for other jobs. I'm not going to lie about that. But there wasn't anything even close to comparable. I stayed for selfish reasons mostly, and because I told Brett if he ever said anything like that to me again, I'd tell my brother and he'd cut Brett's dick off with a bowie knife before he filleted him like a fish."

That knocks me back in my seat. "Would your brother really have . . ."

"If you had a brother, wouldn't he?" she replies.

"Did you tell your brother?" I ask, a thought dawning.

Her eyes widen. "No. Oh my God. No. He had nothing to do with Brett's death. I swear on my grandmother's grave."

"I didn't mean it to be accusatory. I just—"

Temperance shakes her head. "No, I'd be asking

the same question if I were you. Besides, if I'd told my brother, Brett would've been dead a whole lot sooner. Not that that's any comfort. *Shit*. I shouldn't have said that. I'm so sorry. I'm such a bitch." She rises halfway out of the chair, as if preparing to flee my office.

"Stop. Sit. It's fine." I can barely process the conversation we're having, but I decide to tell her something very few people know. "I was already in the process of leaving Brett when it happened. I mean, it still hurt like hell to lose him because of what I thought we had in the beginning. I'm sure it comes as no surprise to you that he was cheating on me."

Temperance returns to her seat, sympathy creasing her features. "I'm so sorry. For all of it. For men being dicks. For the fact that you had to deal with everything that happened."

"It's not your fault."

She lifts her glass. "Not yours either. To the good men out there who still exist, even if they're not perfect and sometimes a little downright bad."

I raise my glass and we touch the rims together again, but her toast sends my brain into a tailspin. I assume she's talking about her brother, but the *downright bad* piece applies thoroughly to Mount.

I drain the glass, knowing it will be my last. Any more and I'll contemplate running again so I don't have to face him, and that's not an option.

No, tonight we need to hammer out the terms of this bargain since he walked out on me last time.

I lower my empty glass to the desk and meet Temperance's gaze. "Thank you for being honest with me, although I wish you'd told me as soon as it happened. I totally get why you didn't. Thank you for sticking it out when you shouldn't have, because I couldn't have made it through these last few months without you. You're definitely going to get that raise."

Temperance's smile is warm and genuine, just like she is. "I love this job. I love this company, and I'm proud to work here." She rises from the chair again. "Just so you know, you're an incredible boss."

Her words fill me with pride, but on the flip side, I think about how easily she could have had a totally different boss today. One who was brutal. One she wouldn't be proud to work for. Actually, Mount probably would have chained the doors shut with no warning, and all my employees would be looking for new jobs.

This is why I agreed, I tell myself.

"Thank you. That means a lot coming from you." I hope she knows how sincere my words are.

"I better head back to my office to work for another hour before I drive home. Better safe than sorry, right?"

"Smart girl."

"I try. See you tomorrow, boss." Temperance heads for the door, leaving the remainder of the champagne behind.

It's beyond tempting. How easy would it be for me to get drunk enough that I wouldn't remember anything that happens tonight? But I'm not going to do it. I already have a buzz, and that's enough of a disadvantage as far as I'm concerned.

I push up from my chair and take the bottle into

the bathroom, dumping its contents down the drain before my better judgment slips away. I leave the empty on the counter. I'll worry about recycling it tomorrow with the rest of the restaurant's glass. Tonight, I have a lot bigger things to worry about.

I gather my things and slip my purse over my shoulder before heading toward the door, already gathering the courage I need to face Mount after the scene this afternoon.

As I reach the threshold, a vibration zips through my bag and I freeze.

The toy.

Shit.

I spin around, leaning my shoulders against the door.

"Is that a warning because you know I haven't put it back in yet, or are you trying to get me pissed off before I'm 'delivered' to you again?" I ask the question to the empty room that I'm not so certain is empty anymore. I know he's not here, but I can't help but wonder.

"Are you watching me right now, you controlling son of a bitch? Where are the cameras?" I turn around, the champagne and fuck-me heels making me unsteady as I search the office I thought I knew inside and out. "Where are they?" I say it just loud enough not to draw attention from Temperance in her office down the hall.

I step toward the door again, and the vibrator buzzes in my purse before I can touch the handle. I step away from the closed door and walk to the center of the room, my steps steady and measured this time. I put my middle fingers in the air and turn in a slow circle.

"Let me know if you can see that, Mount."

The device in my purse is still, but something tells me he's watching me.

I stalk to the bathroom, slam the door, and throw my purse on the counter. It smacks into the champagne bottle, sending it rolling off the edge.

"Shit!"

The mouth of the bottle lands at an angle on the floor, breaking into two pieces at the neck.

That could have been way worse, I tell myself as I reach down to grab the broken pieces of glass.

With my slight buzz from the champagne, I misjudge and the jagged edge of half the bottle slashes diagonally across my left palm.

"Fuck!"

Blood drips from my skin, and it stings like a son of a bitch. I grab a paper towel from the dispenser and squeeze my hand shut around it to staunch the bleeding as I crouch down to root around under the sink for the first aid kit. I know there's one in here somewhere. My father's motto is *Always be prepared*, which makes sense because he was an Eagle Scout. Another tradition he wanted to pass along to a son he was never blessed with.

I find the first aid kit and grab a roll of gauze and some tape. Apparently always being prepared doesn't include palm-sized bandages in the kit. I lift the paper towel off the slice and wince, although it's not as bad as it first seemed. It definitely hurts, but it doesn't look like it's deep enough to need stitches.

Thank the Lord, because the feel of sutures tugging

at my skin while a doctor sews me up, even if I'm numb, creeps me the hell out.

I wrap the roll of gauze around my hand and cover it with tape to hold it in place. The broken bottle I'll deal with tomorrow when I'm totally sober. I grab my purse and stalk out of my office, ready to be *collected*.

SEVENTEEN

Keira

I T'S NOT UNTIL I'M HOODED IN THE BACKSEAT OF THE car driven by Scar that my purse begins buzzing. As soon as it does, my stomach drops at the memory of what Mount told me this morning.

"*This better be in your pussy when you're delivered to me.*"

The incident with the champagne bottle, and field dressing the resulting wound, totally made me forget why I walked into the bathroom to begin with. I have a feeling he won't believe my story.

Shit. I consider my options as the car heads who knows where.

I can reach into my purse, blinded by the hood, and try to maneuver this thing into myself one-handed while Scar no doubt watches me in the rearview mirror. Or I can face Mount knowing I disobeyed a direct order and own up to it.

I'm tempted to flash my goods in the car. I really

am. I reach into my purse with my uninjured hand and wrap it around the toy that's continually pulsing and vibrating.

That asshole wants me writhing in the back of his driver's car? Guaranteed he's expecting me to be on the brink when I'm delivered. Maybe he thinks it'll make me more compliant.

He doesn't know me at all. That seals my decision—I'm not doing it. I won't sacrifice my dignity to follow his order and shove a sex toy into myself while someone else is watching. Not happening.

The drive seems to take forever, but I think it's the hood messing with me. Stealing my sense of sight screws with my head, which I'm sure Mount intends. Unless he's just that secretive about where he lives that no one else can know. Which means he's either a manipulative son of a bitch, a paranoid one, or both.

Before I can decide, Scar comes to a complete stop, and I recognize the sound of the car shifting into park before he kills the engine.

The driver's door opens, and just like all the other times, mine is opened as well. I'm lifted into his arms, and this time, my purse comes with me.

I have to wonder about Scar's daily workout routine if he carries me all over like I weigh nothing, which certainly isn't the case. Tits and ass and drinking more than a little whiskey add extra pounds on a girl, but I couldn't care less.

Magnolia's words come back to me.

"You got tits, ass, and that gorgeous red hair that makes a man think he's gonna find fire when he gets you

*under him . . . And what's more, you're totally and com-
pletely oblivious to it."*

As I'm carried up, down, and all over hell and
back, I realize Mount said something similar.

*"You're totally fucking clueless about what men
think when they look at you. Except today. Today, you
felt it."*

It's true that I don't spend an inordinate amount
of time staring at my reflection in a mirror. Mostly
because I'm too damn busy working. I never got into
the whole selfies and social media thing, and don't
take them unless someone forces me into a picture for
some work-related reason.

I didn't place much stock in what Magnolia said.
I know my friend wouldn't lie to me, but she saw me
through the lens of friendship, and that adds beauty
you may not otherwise see to a person.

But what Mount said earlier today? That got
through to me. Normally, I was clueless. I didn't expect
or notice stares from men. That was more Jury's territory. Or even Imogen, with her perfect features and
undeniably classic beauty.

I was the one following my dad to work, learning
about the variations in flavors we could create by ag-
ing the whiskey in different kinds of barrels, or which
grain suppliers were preferable and why.

Except today . . . today, Mount was right. I felt every stare as those men basically conducted our entire
business meeting with my nipples instead of my eyes.
It was humiliating, not gratifying.

Another sin to lay at his feet. Which is probably

where he'll crush me tonight when he learns I didn't follow his orders.

My musings are cut short when I'm placed on my stilettos, and the sound of a door shutting and locking invades my brain. Like last time, I rip the hood off my head and am poised to attack as I absorb my surroundings. It's like wondering if you're going to be left in a room with a ravenous tiger or a meek housecat.

The analogy holds way too much truth for me to contemplate as I swivel and take in the same sitting room I left this morning. It looks the same, minus the silver-dome-covered trays that I left untouched. I barely touched my lunch either, except for the whiskey.

Both of those things explain why that champagne went to my head even faster than normal.

I walk into the bedroom, again on guard, waiting and wondering from which direction Mount is going to pounce, but a search of each room turns up nothing.

He may be watching me, but he's not doing it from inside this room. When I set my purse down on the nightstand, I'm reminded of the toy inside it rather than inside *me*, where it's supposed to be.

I have a decision to make. *Comply or rebel.*

Magnolia's advice was not to let him walk all over me. Right now, my hand aches like a bitch, and the last thing I want to do is touch that thing. *So, screw it.* What's the worst he can do to me?

Actually, I don't want to know the answer to that question.

Still, so far, all I've been subjected to is the loss of my freedom, which royally pisses me off, but he hasn't caused me any physical harm. I've even had a couple of orgasms.

Maybe I can go toe-to-toe with Mount and come out unscathed.

It doesn't take long before I realize I'm dead wrong.

EIGHTEEN

Keira

THERE'S ONE THING HANGING IN THE MASSIVE walk-in closet, a black silk dress with a deep V that looks like it'll barely cover my boobs. Slits run up both sides to the hip. I look around for matching lingerie, but there's nothing. I check every drawer in the center island, but they're all empty. So, basically, he expects me to look like a classy slut for dinner. *Great.*

Something gold catches my eye as it dangles from the hanger of the dress. A gold chain with a single charm in the shape of a tiny, delicate lock. A symbol of my captivity? Like I need the reminder.

When I pull the dress from the hanger, a note floats to the floor, and I reach down to pick it up.

Change immediately.
Keep your pussy full.

The arrogance of his voice rings through my head

as I read his scrawled words.

Go fuck yourself is the first thought that follows. Right now, I'm nursing my hand and a buzz, and I'm not willing to fall into line like everyone else in Mount's life. Maybe it's the champagne making me bold, but I like to think it's not, because I'm definitely not drunk. If I were drunk, I'd be numb from the pain.

And not just the pain in my hand. Temperance telling me what Brett tried to get her to do shredded me.

My eyes sting with tears as I lean against the center island to hold myself up. I'm tempted to crumple in the closet and give in to them. Only one thing stops me. Or I should say *one man*.

"Are you incapable of following simple directions? Because I thought you were smarter than that."

I jerk my head up to see Mount standing in the doorway that leads to the bathroom, once again making one of his stupid silent entrances.

"How do you do that? And why?" Frustrated, I let out a huff. "You know what? Don't answer. I don't care. Tonight, I'm not in the mood to deal with your brand of arrogant bullshit. I am fresh out of fucks to give."

With each word I speak, his expression darkens with malevolence, telling me I've crossed into dangerous territory.

"What did you fucking say to me?"

Fight or die trying. Isn't that what I vowed to do?

"I said, I'm not in the mood."

He takes a step into the closet and shuts the door behind him. I don't know if it's a power play or what, but instantly the room seems to shrink to a tenth of its size.

"Say it again," he orders.

I stand straight and meet his black glare. "I'm not in the fucking mood to deal with another asshole tonight. Okay?" I throw my hands into the air like I'm completely at a loss of how to deal with him. Which I truly am.

Mount's expression transforms from anger to rage in the space of a single heartbeat, and his voice drops to a low, raspy whisper. "Who fucking touched you? Heads will roll, and I'll swing the goddamned ax myself."

Before I know what's happening, he reaches out with lightning speed and his hand cuffs the wrist of my injured palm.

I'm struggling to keep up with his threats and movements, and definitely regretting the champagne. "What? No one. Well, no one other than you. And I guess Scar when he carries me around like I'm incapable of walking."

"Then what the fuck is this?" He jerks my hand between us, staring down at the gauze and tape.

"Nothing," I say, my voice shaking even though I fight the tremor.

I watch him while he stares at the evidence of my first-aid skills before lifting his gaze to mine. Assessing. Calculating. Judging.

He releases my wrist as quickly as he grabbed it. "Bend over and show me your cunt."

My mouth drops open at his rapid change.

"Now." The word echoes in the closet.

I've never been given a more implacable order in my life, and I've also never quite regretted a decision so much as I do the one I made only minutes ago when I decided not to reinsert the toy.

Determined, I swallow my fear. I was willing to accept my punishment only minutes ago, and I'm not going to lose my nerve now.

Giving him my back, I bend over, lifting my skirt at the same time. It takes him less than a second to see what's missing.

"I gave you an order, a simple fucking order, and you won't even comply with that." He yanks down my skirt. "Stand up."

I do and spin around to face him, not trusting him at my back. "I'm sorry slashing my hand open while I was on my way to follow your damn orders stopped me from playing your little fucking games with my life!"

His expression goes blank as he grabs my wrist again, holding it palm out. "You said it was nothing."

"To you, it's not. That would probably take a severed limb. Or maybe decapitation?"

He drags me by the wrist as he yanks open the closet door and pulls me into the bathroom. He doesn't release me as he digs through the drawers.

"Let go." I jerk my hand, but his grip is like a shackle.

"Not until I see if you're lying to me."

Mount finally produces what look like nail scissors and cuts through the tape and gauze on the back side of my hand. He then peels the bandage free before flipping my hand palm-side up.

His nostrils flare as he surveys the cut, and I have no idea what to expect from him when his dark gaze meets mine.

"How did this happen? No bullshit, Keira. I want the truth."

Saliva pools in my mouth and I swallow it before I explain. "I knocked over the champagne bottle my assistant brought to celebrate our new contract, and it broke on the bathroom floor. When I went to pick it up, I sliced myself on the edge."

His grip on my wrist loosens, and he tilts my hand from side to side in the light. "It doesn't need stitches."

I open my mouth to tell him I already know that, but snap it shut when he runs the pad of his thumb along the same angle as the cut, but a half inch away, careful not to touch it.

"It might leave a scar, though."

I feel his touch like it's bathed in fire, leaving a scorching trail in its wake. My fingers curl inward instinctively, but he stops the motion by covering them with his own.

"Don't. You'll start the bleeding again. Hold still."

When he releases my wrist, I'm confused enough to actually obey. He crouches down and pulls a first aid kit from beneath the sink.

"Just like my father. Always prepared." The words pop out of their own volition.

Mount rises slowly, his dark gaze pinning me in place. "Don't assume I'm anything like your father. You couldn't be any more wrong if you tried."

As he pulls something from the first aid kit, my response flies from my lips. "You're right. My father is a good man, and as far as I can tell, there's not a damn good thing about you."

"Now you're catching on," he says, his wicked smirk intact.

And then something burns like *actual fire* along my cut, and I try to yank my wrist out of his grip. He doesn't let go. Instead, he uses his free hand to fan the searing cut.

"What the hell did you do to me?"

"Calm down. It's liquid Band-Aid. It's more effective on your palm than your hack job with the gauze and tape. It'll stop burning in a second." He continues directing air toward the cut to soothe the pain.

"You could've warned me! That shit hurts!"

Mount's expression goes blank. "I've given you more warnings than I have anyone before. It doesn't seem to be working, though, because you're the most stubborn woman I've ever met. And if you think that hurts, you've never known real pain."

He releases my wrist and replaces the first aid kit while the burning subsides to a manageable sting.

Do I thank him? I'm pondering the question when he rises to his full height, dwarfing me by nearly a foot, something I hadn't noticed until we were forced into such close proximity.

"Get dressed. You're making us late for dinner." He strides from the bathroom, but doesn't leave the bedroom before tossing his parting words over his shoulder. "And don't forget the toy, or I'll take it as a direct invitation to bend you over the dining room table and fuck your tight little cunt while they serve the first course."

NINETEEN

Keira

SHOCKINGLY, MOUNT PULLS OUT MY CHAIR AND pushes it in while I take my seat at the massive dining room table that looks like it could easily seat twenty people. His place setting is at the head, and I've been seated directly to his left.

I don't make eye contact with him as I sit, because I swear the man can read my mind.

To my shame, his parting words made me wet enough that there was no need to search for lube to slide the toy back inside me where he demanded.

What the hell is wrong with me?

I should be disgusted and repulsed. Screaming for someone to let me out of this damn house—which I still haven't gotten to see because Scar hooded me and carried me to dinner. But instead, all I can do is picture Mount grabbing a fistful of my hair and holding it tight while he bends me over the table and mounts me like his name suggests.

Again, what the hell is wrong with me?

There's fucking with someone's head, and then there's what Mount is doing to me. I don't think a name has been invented for it yet. I'm pretty sure it's not Stockholm Syndrome, because I *definitely* hate him and would run in the opposite direction the second I got the chance, if there weren't threats hanging over the heads of my friends and family like guillotine blades. Then there are the two warring parts of me—the one that wants what he threatens, and the one that rebels against every word of it.

"Do I need to check?" Mount's deep voice whispers in my ear as he releases my chair.

Before I can respond, the toy buzzes to life and I jolt in my seat, giving him his answer.

"I didn't think so."

I want to slap that arrogant smirk off his face, but I can't even imagine the consequences for that action. Thankfully, the vibrator stills before the first course is served. By the time I've finished spooning up my oyster soup in silence and it's been cleared away, I know what I have to do.

"We need to talk terms."

The efficient waitstaff serve the salad course before Mount responds. "The only terms to be discussed were those of your willing submission. You agreed. End of discussion."

I drop my fork and the silver clanks against the delicate china plate. I'm too pissed to give proper thought to how strange it is that a man as brutal as Mount would surround himself with such finery.

"No. That's not how negotiations work."

He raises one dark eyebrow at my response, and I have to wonder if that's an ability bestowed only upon arrogant men specifically for moments like this.

"Besides, this conversation is about the end of our bargain. I need to know exactly how long you're going to keep me here, because you're screwing with my life and my business."

The smirk that tugs at the corners of his mouth is one I'm beginning to recognize, and it never precedes anything good for me. "So eager to repay your debt and be done with me?"

"Absolutely." I spit the word out like something foul.

Mount, dressed in a suit that fits him to perfection as usual, rests his forearms on the table and leans in. "There is no *end* to our bargain until I'm done with you."

Rage, my familiar friend, builds in my belly. "And when will that be?" I try to keep the question as civil as possible.

His smirk turns lopsided, throwing fuel on the fire. "I'll make sure to send you notice in writing."

If my eyeballs could shoot flames across the table, Mount would be incinerated in mere moments.

"That's bullshit," I say, my bravery growing.

All traces of humor fade from his face. *Did I cross the line?*

"No, what's bullshit is that my repayment is in the form of pleasure, and I haven't gotten a single fucking bit of it from you yet."

He shoves his chair back from the table, rattling the china and sending water spilling over the edges of our crystal goblets.

"You've got a bum hand, but your mouth sure as hell works." He nods down at his lap. "Get on your knees."

My lungs heave with fury, because the only thing I can picture right now is Brett sitting behind a desk, ordering Temperance to suck his dick in order to get a raise.

They're all the same.

"Go fuck yourself, Mount. I'll never get on my knees for you." I mean every single word of what may be the most dangerous vow I've ever made.

A muscle in his jaw flexes as his nostrils flare. A server enters the room quietly, no doubt to check to see if we're ready for the next course.

"Get the fuck out."

His order sends adrenaline dumping into my bloodstream, because he never drops his gaze from mine. I shove away from the table, ready to run. *I thought I was a stand-and-fight girl, but it turns out I'm more of a flight girl.*

The server disappears, shutting the door with a decisive click, but I don't even clear my chair before Mount slams his palm on the table, making the china jump.

"Not you. You're not leaving this room until I get what I want. You made the deal; you honor the deal. *Willingly.*"

"I hate you." The truth rings in all three words.

"Then I guess we're gonna have a lot of hate-fucking until I'm done with you."

The vibrator springs to life at the highest, most intense setting. It pulsates inside me, adding a surge of lust to the maelstrom of emotions rioting through me, overwhelming everything else.

"How long do I let it go before I stop it and deny you?" His question is rhetorical, and besides, I'm incapable of answering. "As many times as I've been denied access to that sweet cunt? Or until you beg me to come?"

My fingers curl into the lace-and-linen tablecloth as I try to hold on to some semblance of my sanity.

How can I want this man? I hate him.

But I've never craved anyone more.

He changes the settings over and over, driving me to the edge and stopping each time right before I come. I'm ready to scream in frustration because it's only a matter of moments before I break, and I refuse to let him bring me to my knees, literally or figuratively.

"Just fuck me already and let me come, you sadistic son of a bitch!" The shrill voice echoes in the massive room, and I hardly recognize it as my own.

"Fucking finally," he says, and I'm too far gone to care about the triumph in his tone. Mount rips the tablecloth aside, sending the china and crystal crashing to the floor.

He reaches for me at the same moment I step toward him. Both of his hands reach out and lock around my waist, yanking me closer before lifting me onto the table between his spread legs.

Mount doesn't bother with the slit in the dress. He shreds the delicate silk down the center, starting right at the deep V neckline, until it floats to the floor in tatters. His massive hand closes around my neck, and he presses me down until my spine touches the table.

"You push me to the edge like no woman ever has, and now I'm going to fuck you like I've planned from day one. The way you've been dying to be fucked your whole life."

"Arrogant bastard." My words are quiet, muted by his hold on me, even though he's not even remotely cutting off my air supply.

"I'm ruthless, not arrogant, and you're about to learn the difference."

Mount withdraws the hand at my throat to rip off his suit coat and then tugs the toy from my body. He holds it up, once again in obvious satisfaction because it's dripping from me.

"You fucking love this. You don't just want it, you need it. And I'm the only man who's going to give it to you."

He shoves down the zipper of his pants and the top button goes flying. I don't get a chance to see his cock before he buries it to the hilt with a single thrust.

"More." That plea can't be falling from my lips. I would never beg like that.

I'm aware of nothing but the wild lust surging higher and faster as he stretches me to the point where pleasure blurs with pain, and it sends me soaring. My inner muscles clamp down, and in a single moment,

I'm no longer lying flat on my back on the dining room table, but instead I'm wrapped around him and tearing off his shirt like he shredded my dress. Any thought of my injured hand is obliterated as I dig my nails into his shoulders and claw at him like a wild animal in heat as my orgasm crashes through me with more ferocity than anything I've ever experienced.

Mount growls as his hands drop to my ass, gripping my cheeks as he lifts me off the table and pumps into me over and over. I don't know or care if I'm leaving marks, but I'll be damned if I beg him for anything again, especially to let me come. I close my teeth over the thick muscle of his shoulder in an attempt to muffle my screams.

I fail, but there's no way Mount can hear it over his own roar as his cock pulses inside me, spilling his release.

As soon as I can form a rational thought, it's—

Holy fuck, we didn't use a condom.

TWENTY

Mount

THE FIRE IN THAT WOMAN IS UNMATCHED. IT ONLY required the right tinder and spark. Luckily for me, I learned the basics early on—flint, steel, and paper stolen from the butcher's Dumpster. It was enough to keep me warm on the rare nights it got cold enough to freeze this city.

If I'd had Keira Kilgore, there would have been no need, because together we would have burned this town to ash.

You know what happens when you throw gasoline on a fire? You get a raging inferno, and that's what happened tonight.

At least until I pulled out and my cum dripped from between her legs.

Fuck.

I've never gone without a condom, even in the days when I shoplifted them because I didn't want to choose between sex and food.

Keira looks at me like I just put the spawn of the devil inside her, and maybe she's not that far off. "Why would you do that? How could you not use a condom?"

She's making this out to be my fault? Obviously, because when the devil's in the room, who else could there possibly be to blame?

"I planned to bury my cock in your throat and make you swallow every drop, but you fucked that up all by yourself."

The mouth in question, the one that still hasn't touched my dick, drops open. "You're saying this is my fault?" She points to herself and shakes her head. "You're such an asshole."

No other woman would dare toss as many slurs at me as she has, but for some reason, it amuses me. *Most of the time.*

"Well, at least I'm the asshole who's always worn a condom. You're not catching shit from me. You can trust me on that."

"Trust you? Never!"

My temper blazes out of control. I just came harder than ever before in my life, with the woman who made me wait the longest, and I don't even get to enjoy it for more than a few seconds after my dick stopped pulsing because she's losing her shit over this condom business.

Then another thought occurs to me. I'll admit, I could have handled it better, but the woman pushes me to the edge.

"I'm more worried about what I could catch from you. Your shit-bag husband fucked anything that moved."

Her indrawn breath borders on homicidal, and given her temper, I'm not ruling it out as a possibility. Especially because she can't form actual words to reply.

"At least tell me you're on the pill. Having a fucking kid is *not* in my plans." I've never taken such a stupid risk before. A kid would be the ultimate weakness.

Finally, Keira's able to speak. "Thank God I have an IUD and we don't have to worry about that."

The way she says it infuriates me to the point where my temper turns ice cold. If I lash out right now, she'll never recover. So, like the devil masquerading as a gentleman, I grab my suit coat off the chair and toss it to her.

"Cover yourself up. No one sees those tits, that ass, or that pussy but me."

Her green eyes blaze like melting emeralds. She wraps the coat around her body, straightening that steel spine with her unbreakable pride again.

"Go fuck yourself, Mount. Because that's the only way you're coming again in this bargain."

At that moment, I'm so far beyond anger, the urge to laugh at her comment rattles through me, but I don't. She stalks from the room, wearing my suit coat like a grain sack and nothing else. V will be outside the door, ready to escort her back to her room, so that's not something I have to worry about.

No, the only things I have to concern myself with are how fucking wrong she is, and how I'm going to find a way into that tight pussy again. The alternative is not an option, and her willingness is non-negotiable. That's one thing I won't compromise on.

When I step into the palatial shower in my master bath a half hour later, the only thought on my mind is how fucking sweet it's going to be when I get what I want. Again. And again. Keira can lie to herself all she wants, but I know the truth.

"Fuck." I bite out the curse as I step under the spray, and water hits the teeth marks on my shoulder and the claw marks on my back left by my little Irish hellion despite her earlier injury.

She was fucking magnificent. No, not past tense. *Is.* Even as she walked away wearing nothing but my coat, she held her head high and proud. Most men won't look me in the eye, but this woman isn't afraid to declare all-out war.

If she thinks her cursing me to hell is going to make me more likely to let her go, she's delusional. She amuses me. Challenges me. And goddamn, she enrages me to the point where the only thing I can do is fuck her into submission. Which, luckily for both of us, she needs, whether she realizes it yet or not.

I replay the scene in my head from tonight, from the moment she stepped into the dining room in that dress. Her amazing tits on display just the way I wanted them, the slits up both sides of the skirt showing off her legs with every step.

I close my hand around my cock as I picture her walking toward me like a queen deigning to allow a peon an audience.

She calls me arrogant, but every time she raises

that haughty chin of hers, I want to take her over my knee and spank her ass, which makes my dick even harder.

I don't need to get myself off in the shower. It hasn't even been an hour since I came, but I can't stop seeing and hearing her in my head.

"Go fuck yourself, Mount. I'll never get on my knees for you."

Oh, but you will, Keira. You will. *And I will make sure you enjoy every fucking second of it.*

With one hand pressed against the stone wall of the shower, I grip my cock tighter and stroke it as I picture those pissed-off red lips turning pouty and soft after I've gotten her off enough times that she begs me to stop because she can't take any more and promises me anything in return. That's when they'll be wrapped around my cock.

My balls tighten at the mental picture, and I stroke harder and faster.

Fuck, I don't even need her on her knees. She can hang that thick mane of red hair over the edge of the bed, and I'll fuck her face and teach her to take every inch down her throat without gagging.

My cock pulses, my orgasm bearing down faster than I expect considering that I just came. But it's not me. It's the thought of her moaning as she sucks and tongues my shaft every time I pull out until I blow inside her mouth and watch my cum drip from those stubborn lips.

Mine.

As my cum splatters the rock wall in my shower, I

swear to myself it's the last time. She'll never deny me again.

She may have marked me tonight, but I marked her first.

Keira Kilgore needs another lesson in what it means to be owned by Lachlan Mount.

TWENTY-ONE

Keira

WHEN I WAKE THE NEXT MORNING, I BOLT UP IN bed, my head swiveling from side to side. It's the same way I wake up every time in this damn room. Never knowing if I'm going to be alone, or who has been in here during the night. Based on the spinning fireplace in the library that I saw the first time I was delivered to Mount, I know this place is riddled with secret passageways and hidden entrances. That's assuming, I suppose, that the room I'm being kept in is even in the same building as the library. Honestly, I don't know where the hell I am.

This morning, I see no one, and it's a relief. I shift, swinging my legs over the edge of the bed and out from under the covers. Muscles I don't recall having twinge in protest. I try focusing on my sore hand instead, but fail miserably because all I can think about is the ache between my legs. I still feel him pounding into me.

I've only had one sexual encounter in my life that

remotely approached what happened last night, and that was the first time Brett and I were together. It was never that good again. Probably because I married him within twenty-four hours, and he didn't feel the need to expend the effort.

I push that thought aside, but the one that follows doesn't make me feel much better.

I don't know how last night happened. As I stumble into the massive bathroom, I feel *taken. Owned. Used.* But not in a bad way. Or maybe just not the bad way I expected.

I move toward the shower and reach inside to flip the handle to hot. I spent a half hour in there last night, determined to scrub his touch from my body, but it didn't work.

I still feel him on every inch of me.

While I wait for the water to heat, I brush out my tangled mass of hair. I'm beginning to get used to my nakedness, something I've never been comfortable with before. I suppose it's because I have no clothes and, therefore, no other option.

I put that item on my agenda for today. This one-outfit-at-a-time bullshit has to end.

When I lower the brush to the countertop, I catch a glimpse of something in my reflection. My hip. And around the sides of my ass.

I spin, craning my neck over my shoulder to look behind me, and I see it.

Or rather *them*. Light bruises in the shape of fingerprints.

That asshole *marked* me. I wait for the expected

fury to burn in my gut, and it does, right on schedule. In my head, I'm already calling him every foul name I can come up with as I step into the shower.

I can't scrub these off, and I can't block out the memories either.

I hate that they pummel me like the hot spray.

My anger drains away and shame replaces it when I realize I can't even stay pissed about the marks, because under no circumstances can I say I was unwilling last night. I urged him on as he gripped my hips and fucked me harder.

That asshole got his wish.

He manipulated me. Messed with my head. But there's no doubt that I begged him for it in the end.

Shame burns down my face in two hot streams that I refuse to admit are tears. I'm getting better and better at lying to myself.

I slap my palms against the shower wall and hang my head between them, letting the water pour over me. *Wash me clean. Absolve me of the sins I've committed.*

After several long minutes, I let loose a final sniffle and stand straight with my new mantra for the day pounding in my head with the same intensity I still feel between my thighs.

Lachlan Mount will not break me. He might fuck me. He might fuck with my head. But he will never break me.

I use the back of my hands to wipe at my eyes and swear to myself that he will never earn another one of my tears. He's not worth it. I hate him.

The intensity of my feelings hasn't faded. It grows

stronger each time my body turns against me. It's humiliating that I find so much pleasure in what he does to me. I'm sure he's plenty amused by it.

A spine of steel won't help me with Mount. Titanium is required.

The only person who can decide who and what humiliates me is *me*, and I won't give him that power ever again.

Fuck him.

Which I know I'll do, even though everything in me wants to deny it.

Magnolia said there's nothing wrong with enjoying it, but she's never dealt with Mount before. Or has she?

I remember my purse in the bedroom. Scar didn't take it from me last night, but I was too furious to even think to use my phone.

The first thing I'm going to do when I get out of this shower is text Magnolia. She might not get up before noon, but a late-afternoon lunch with her just became imperative. I have to know if there's anything else she's managed to uncover since this whole disaster began.

I need more ammunition against Mount if I'm going to win this battle, not to mention anything possible to armor myself against him. Magnolia told me not to let him get into my head, and I'm failing at that task about as spectacularly as America's war on drugs.

Magnolia will help me. She'll have wisdom to impart. If nothing else, talking to her will be another piece of normalcy I can reclaim.

When I turn off the shower fifteen minutes later and wrap myself in one of the luxuriously thick and fluffy towels hanging on the warmer, tucking one end between my breasts, my entire body stills as I reach for a second one to dry my hair.

I'm no longer alone.

Mount leans indolently against the door frame that leads to the bedroom.

My first thought is one of utter invasion. "Now I don't even get to shower in private?"

"You get what I give you. Nothing more, nothing less."

I force my limbs to break free from their paralysis and grab the second towel like nothing is amiss and wrap it turban-style around my head. "Can you lay off the clichés? It's too early for that crap."

I turn toward the mirror, determined to ignore his presence, but fail. Out of the corner of my eye, I swear he's fighting off a smile.

"What? Not going to throw in it's nothing you haven't seen before? That I'm nothing special?" I don't know why I'm taunting him. Probably because he's making me absolutely crazy.

I peer into the glass, pretending to look at my pores as I reach down for the high-end skin-care products I was provided, but my hand misses the bottle because I'm too distracted by his face and the constantly changing expressions on it. They're too swift to get a lock on, and I wish I could read his mind as easily as he seems to read mine.

"The steam was too thick to see through the glass. I wasn't sure you were ever going to get out of the damned shower. Still feel me?"

One of the bottles goes flying as I spin around. "Go fuck yourself."

This time, the smile that forms is harsh and forbidding. "I did that last night in my own shower, and I won't fucking do it again, because I've got you here to take care of my every need."

I can only imagine how I would have spit and clawed if he'd summoned me after our last confrontation to give him a handy in the shower.

"In your dreams."

His smile shifts, now baring his teeth. "Hurry up. You've got a meeting with your banker this morning to discuss how close you are to tripping your loan covenants and being handed off to the workout department as one of the bank's troubled assets."

My mouth falls open. "How do you know that?"

He scoffs. "I find the fact that you think I wouldn't even more insulting."

"What time is it?" I glance around but it's pointless because there's not a single clock in this damn cell. It's like being in a casino but without all the fun and a hell of a lot more risk.

"You have less than an hour to make it on time. So, I suggest you hurry."

"Fuck." I let out the curse, and yes, I know it's not ladylike, but I was raised around men working in a distillery. "Then get the hell out so I can."

I expect another imperious glare or smug grin followed by him telling me he doesn't have to do a damned thing, but instead he pushes off the door frame and disappears into the master bedroom.

Shocking, actually. And more worrisome than I want to admit.

I rush through getting ready, trying to make sure my face looks as professional as possible before I hurry into the closet to find, of course, only one outfit waiting for me.

This time it's a wrap dress made of silky fabric in stark black. The same color of Mount's perfectly tailored suit. *Not that I noticed or anything.*

And, miracle of miracles, there's a matching black thong and a black bra that plunges in the middle, perfectly suited to the neckline of the dress. The same gold chain and lock dangles on the hanger from the night before.

I ignore it. He didn't notice I wasn't wearing it last night, so maybe he won't notice this morning. Not wearing it might be petty, but if it helps me retain another shred of control, I'll take it.

I slide on an expensive pair of black pumps with gold trim around the soles and heels and stride into the bedroom, expecting to find Mount waiting on the bed. But he isn't. I find him in the sitting room, lounging on an armless chair next to the table where the covered trays were yesterday. Those are absent today as well.

"Shit, my coat." I turn around to dash back into the bedroom to grab it and then head straight for the door that leads out of my cage.

"Aren't you forgetting an accessory?" Mount asks.

The damn necklace. Of course he has to make it an issue.

"Fine."

I spin on a heel, pissed that I'm giving in to him, but telling myself it's only because I can't be late for this meeting. It's not an option.

Mount was right. My loan officer is pissed that we're only paying the minimum payment on our line of credit every month, even as we continue to borrow. Today is my chance to convince him that the check coming in from the Voodoo Kings will take a big enough chunk out of what we owe to keep Seven Sinners from being labeled "troubled." The last place I want our loan to end up is in the hands of a workout officer, who will basically tell me I need to liquidate, pay off the debt I owe the bank, and walk away. I've already sold my body to the devil to save Seven Sinners, and now I might have to offer my soul to the bank to keep it running.

I grab the necklace and realize the lock isn't just a charm; it actually holds the two ends of the chain together.

Like a freaking collar.

Are you kidding me right now? I want to rebel against this more than anything, but I don't have the time. I also don't have the key. But I guarantee I know who does.

I walk into the sitting room and hold it out. "I can't put it on. It needs a key."

Mount's hand disappears into his suit jacket pocket and raises a tiny flash of gold, and I hand the chain over to him.

"So compliant this morning, despite your earlier attitude."

"Because I don't have time to waste on you. I have

more important things to worry about."

Mount's expression turns darkly amused. "You have no idea how wrong that statement is. You need to learn who your real adversaries are, girl."

"Don't call me that."

"I'll call you whatever I fucking want." He unlocks the necklace. "Turn around."

I swivel, giving him my back, and stupidly, I'm not afraid of what he could do to me. I should be. I *need* to be. But that fear would be all-consuming, even more so than the man himself, and my refusal to cower will not change.

Mount's fingers, ridiculously hot against my skin, drag along the lines of my collarbone until the chain rests a few inches from my throat. The click is nearly inaudible when he snaps the lock in place, but his touch heightens my awareness as he spins the necklace around so the lock hangs in the front.

"Don't even bother trying to take it off without the key. It won't break."

My smart mouth and sharp tongue beg to argue with him, but I don't have time. "Fine. Whatever. Now, where's Scar and the hood so I can get to work?"

Another smile stretches across Mount's lips. "You're missing your final accessory."

Oh my fucking God. If he means that vibrator, I might murder him, but then again, time is of the essence.

"Where is it?" My question is snappish at best, bitchy at worst.

Mount's grin turns lazier as he holds out another

black box, but this one looks different from yesterday's. A cold shroud settles around me as he lifts the lid to reveal what's inside.

Oh, hell no.

There are things I just won't do. I may not be a good girl, like perfect Imogen, but I'm not a bad girl like Jury either. And I *never have and never will* open my back door for business.

"No." My denial is implacable as I stare down at the black-and-gold butt plug nestled in black velvet.

Mount's grip tightens on the box. "You need to re-move that fucking word from your vocabulary when you're dealing with me. It'll save you a lot of grief."

"No. Fucking. Way," I say, emphasizing each word. "That is not going in me."

Mount's dark gaze burns into me. "Did you not understand when I told you I'd be making use of your hands, mouth, tits, cunt, and ass? Because that's non-negotiable. You agreed. *Willingly.*"

I swallow another sharp reply. My ass is virgin ter-ritory, and I intended for it to remain virgin territory until I was interred in the family burial vault.

"Tick. Tock. Time is running short, Keira. You want to make your meeting or miss it? Because I happen to know for a fact that Lloyd Bunt isn't going to give you a chance to reschedule before he hands your file over to the workout department. Then you'll have to let me taint your pure little body to save your precious compa-ny, and it's going to go down the drain anyway."

"I fucking hate you." The words come out on a sin-gle breath.

"Doesn't make a damn bit of difference to me," he replies, his smile never faltering, but his eyes flash again. "You said you won't go to your knees for me to fuck your mouth, and I've already had your pussy. Your tits aren't going to quite do it for me today, so that leaves only one option. Don't tell me you've never had a cock buried in your ass. Based on the fear in your eyes and the way your pulse is hammering in your neck, I'd swear the answer is no."

I shake my head, refusing to let him make me feel like there's something wrong with me for not trying anal. "And I'm not going to today either."

"Willingly," he repeats, and I want to take back the promise I made.

Mount snaps the lid closed and shoves the box toward me. My hands instinctively close around the edges, and I step out of his reach.

"My cock won't fit in that tight little ass with the stick you've got shoved up it, so we better get to stretching it out." He nods toward the bathroom. "The lube is in the bottom right drawer. My advice? Be generous with it. And you're not leaving without that plug in your ass, so you better hurry if you want to make your meeting."

Rage. My seemingly constant companion blooms again as I back away from the man that I definitely could pull a trigger on, especially at this moment. No one would miss him. New Orleans would rejoice at his demise. Or so I assume.

I keep my steps measured and my glare intact until my heels click on the marble floor of the bathroom and

I slam the door behind me.

Resting my forehead against it for only a few seconds, I stare down at the black box in my hands, and like I've suddenly developed X-ray vision, I can see exactly what lies inside.

When I shove off the panel and face the mirror, my face is the picture of outrage and horror. Which pretty accurately conveys how I feel right now.

I can't do this. The girl in the mirror is one hundred percent certain of that fact. The voice that harnesses my rage argues in opposition. *Of course you can. It's a butt plug, not a syringe of heroin. Stop being a pussy and find the lube so you can go meet your bankers and act like the CEO you are.*

Crouching down, I yank open the bottom right drawer and find the lube exactly where he said it would be. *Fucking bastard.* The slur is getting repetitive, even to my ears. I need to come up with something new to fully express this level of fury.

I snap open the lid of the box and pull out the plug, holding it in one hand and the lube in the other.

All I have to do is spread it on and shove it in. I can do this.

My back door clenches tightly, delivering a solid *no way in hell* response.

But if I miss this meeting and Seven Sinners' loan ends up in workout, my dad will find out, and . . . I don't even want to picture the fallout.

I flip the cap on the lube and dump some on the black-and-gold plug. It doesn't take a genius to figure out how to use it, and I'm pretty sure Magnolia had given me an anal trainer kit years ago as a gag gift that wasn't really a gag.

With the base of the lube-coated plug gripped in one hand and the other tugging down the waistband of my thong, I stare into the mirror and give myself another pep talk.

Just shove it in. I squeeze my eyes shut and awkwardly maneuver it beneath the skirt of my dress, wishing I'd thought to remove it. I press the end against the hole I swore would remain virginal and try to force myself to push, but I can't.

I just can't.

With a cry of disgust, I throw the plug in the sink, tug my thong back into place, and grip the edge of the counter with both hands.

I'm a coward. *And I totally should've used that anal trainer kit.*

There's a knock on the door. "This is your twenty-minute warning. With traffic, you might still make it on time if you hurry."

Glaring, I spin around, wishing once again my stare could incinerate. I dash forward and yank the door open so quickly that I take Mount by surprise. He hangs on to the top edge of the door frame, staring down at me with that arrogant eyebrow raised. He studies me for a moment.

"Turn around and bend over."

"No."

His expression goes dark but flares with interest at the same time. "You and that word. Are you really disobeying my order?"

I swallow, because there's no way I want to admit to him that I can't do it. I hate this weakness in myself almost as much as I hate him. But the clock is ticking, and I don't have time for my pride to get in the way of losing my family's legacy. I've already sacrificed too much.

"I'm not doing it."

His eyes narrow on my face, and he's reading me too easily for comfort—again.

"Oh yes, you are, but that's not what you're saying. You won't let yourself miss this meeting. So it's either you can't or won't. Which one, Keira? Are you being stubborn or shy?" His eyes flare with heat as though both options excite him.

"Does it matter?"

"More than you know."

When I hesitate to respond, he looks down at his watch, and I'm reminded of the need to get the hell out of here as quickly as possible. That's the only thing needed to prompt my honesty.

"I can't."

The darkness fades from his expression, and his black gaze flashes with heat. "Ask me."

He doesn't have to elaborate because I know exactly what he wants. Any other morning, I'd tell him to go fuck himself again, but I don't have that luxury today.

"I need help." I utter the words with the same enthusiasm as I would if I were confessing to murder. Well, anyone's murder but his.

"Help with what, Keira?"

Oh, this motherfucker.

"I hate you."

"It's hard to forget when you constantly tell me. And to be honest, I'm getting sick of hearing it. Now, fucking ask me for exactly what you need."

I jerk my head toward the sink. "Help me put that *thing* in."

"Help you slide that butt plug in your tight little ass so I can stretch it out and then fuck it because it'll make you come harder than you ever knew was possible?"

I grit my teeth, and for the first time in my life, I'm the slightest bit curious if what he's saying is true. Magnolia swore I was missing out, hence the anal trainer kit.

He's fucking with my head again. That's all.

I shove my curiosity down before I bite out my reply. "Yes."

His smug smile of satisfaction appears as if on cue and he walks to the sink. "I can't say you didn't at least try."

He leans down to open the bottom drawer where I'd found the lube and produces some kind of spray and a neatly folded towel, and drops them both beside the sink.

"Clean it. Bring the plug and the lube into the sitting room."

I can't meet my own eyes in the mirror as I wash the plug, and then use the disinfectant spray and wipe it clean. I'm not sure if that's because I can't face my shame or because I'm afraid I'll see a glimmer of excitement.

There's no doubt that Mount's orders affect me like

some kind of black magic. My hard nipples, visible against the fabric of the dress, and the wetness coating my thong are proof of that.

Still, I carry the plug and the lube through the bedroom and into the living room like I'm stepping up to the scaffold to face the noose. Mount is seated in the same chair he was before, but this time, he's moved it farther away from the table.

I cross the plush carpet, my palms beginning to sweat as I stop two feet in front of him and hold out the items. He takes them from me and I start to turn around, already predicting that he'll command me to bend over.

"Stop."

His order stills my movement, and slowly, I look over my shoulder at him. "What?"

"Let me see your hand."

I'm shocked that he gives my injury a second thought. "It's fine. I'm fine."

I flash it at him, intending to tuck it back beside me so we can get this over with, but he grabs my wrist. He surveys the injury for a moment before looking up at me.

"You'll be fine. Should barely feel it by tomorrow."

"I know. I—" Before I can finish telling him I didn't need his assessment, he cuts me off with another order that throws me completely off-balance.

"Over my lap."

I jerk my head back and stare at him like he's insane. "You have to be joking."

His eyes narrow, and my comment sounds

ludicrous even to me. Mount doesn't joke.

"Fine." I attempt to hold tight to my pride, but it's already unraveling as I bend over his lap like a naughty child who earned a spanking.

His palm brushes the back of my thigh, and I jerk at his touch. It's only by biting my lip that I stay silent as he pushes the skirt of the dress up and folds it over my back, completely baring my thong-clad ass to him.

I'm expecting him to be cold and callous in this exercise, but nothing could be further from the truth. His fingers trace the faint bruises I saw in the shower, and my skin heats.

"Do they hurt?"

The question catches me off guard. "Like you would really care."

His palm cups the curve of my ass cheek and squeezes enough to put pressure on the marks. My thighs clamp together involuntarily.

"I want an answer to my question."

"No, okay? It's the curse of fair skin. I bruise easily. It's not a big deal."

"It's lucky for me that I like seeing my marks on you. It's good to know it's so easy and painless to get what I want."

Before I can come up with a sharp reply, he releases his grip and trails a finger up the back of the thong where it's tucked between my cheeks, and they clench together.

He lets out a half laugh at the reaction but never stops his lazy exploration, tucking a fingertip under the waistband and sliding it from side to side.

Every movement is deliberate. He's making me enjoy something I want to hate, and the bulge pressing against my lower belly tells me he's enjoying it just as much. That shouldn't turn me on more, but it does.

"This is the position you'll take when I spank your ass for your constant bad behavior." The remark is offhand, but makes me tense regardless.

"You wouldn't—" I start, but he finishes for me.

"Dare?"

A swat lands against the cheek he cupped, just hard enough to sting before it turns into a heated burn.

"You don't have a fucking clue what I'd dare when it comes to you." He hooks a finger into the waistband and drags my thong down my legs, having to tug to release it from between my clasped thighs.

"Are you already wet for me, Keira?" The question is quiet but carries as much power as one of his roared demands.

When I don't answer right away, he lifts his hips, pressing his hard-on into my belly. There's no way I can miss the thick length of his cock.

"Because I'm hard for you."

I suck in a breath, trying to think of anything that will bring me back to center and make me forget how turned on I am right now. *The meeting.* "I don't have time for this. We have to hurry."

His voice is a low growl when he replies. "You're lucky I want you to make that meeting, or you wouldn't leave this room today. Torturing you with orgasm denial could easily become a new favorite hobby of mine."

I keep my lips pressed together this time, assuming

that the less I speak, the more quickly we'll get it over with, even though my body is screaming at me to enjoy every moment.

Two of his fingers slip between my legs, dragging the pads through my soaked slit and brushing over my clit. I squirm in his lap, desperate to either come or for him to let me free, but I know neither is an option.

"You're so fucking wet for me."

I want to bite out that it's not for him, but again, *time* . . . and the eternal damnation of my soul for lying.

As his fingers play in my wetness, dipping into my opening and tracing around my clit, he murmurs, "You're finally being good. So submissive while I play with this sweet, soaked pussy."

I want to argue that I'm anything but submissive, but he flicks my clit and a charge of pleasure shoots through me. That's when he ups the game, dragging the wetness back toward my ass and lazily dragging a finger around it, coating it with my own slickness. He presses a single finger against the forbidden hole with the lightest pressure, and I tense.

"Relax. I have every intention of making sure you crave this."

His words carry a promise, and I'm terrified that he's going to be proven right. He repeats the process with another finger, the lightest pressure, and my hips press harder against his thighs.

"You can pretend you don't like it, but you love how I play with this tight virgin asshole as much as you loved the way I fucked you on the table last night."

I can't deny it. I've reached the point where words

aren't an option, and if I open my mouth, the only thing that's going to come out is a moan. Besides, if he can make it not hurt when he pushes that plug into my ass, I'm not going to argue. I have retained some small sense of self-preservation.

He switches hands, reaching between my legs to press a long, thick finger into my pussy, fucking it in and out until I'm writhing against him.

He tries a second finger, but the tight channel resists before they both slide in. "It's hard to believe my fat cock fits in this tight little cunt."

I lose track of time as he lazily finger-fucks me and teases my clit. I'm a slave to his deep voice telling me all the dirty things he wants to do to me, and the pleasure he delivers as he does it.

"You're lucky I don't care that you're creaming all over my pants. You're making a mess, Keira." He lowers his head to speak directly into my ear. "Actually, I fucking love it."

I'm beyond the point of shame. I'm as much a willing party to everything that's happening right now as I have been to anything in my life. I want to come so badly that I've lost sight of everything but the goal.

"Please." It's a whisper, and at first I don't realize it's coming from me.

"That word on your lips." He presses hard on my clit before pushing two fingers inside me again. "It's the sexiest thing I've ever heard you say. Except maybe the way you moaned as your pussy clamped down on my cock as you came last night."

His hand never leaves my center, teasing my

entrance and my clit and pushing inside until I'm ready to beg again—but that's when something cool drizzles down my crack and I tense.

"Shhh. It's just lube. I'm going to finger your virgin asshole next, and you're going to love it as much as when I do this." He presses down on my clit, triggering the orgasm that's been building inside me since he started this dangerous game.

Waves of ecstasy wash over me as Mount circles my asshole, adding more pressure with each motion, but he never stops strumming my clit. My brain is divided, unable to keep up with the pleasure and fear at the same time.

"Let me in, Keira. Give me this ass."

Another orgasm builds and when I relax, he breaches the tight ring of muscle with his fingertip. It feels *massive*. Nerve endings that I never knew existed spring to life, and I stiffen again, pushing him out.

"Don't you fucking keep me out of your ass. I own it, I will fuck it, and goddammit, you will let me in."

My second orgasm bursts through me, and his finger pushes all the way inside the virgin hole he's already claimed as his. I'm still riding the waves of pleasure as he pushes it in and out, and I writhe against him, not sure if I'm chasing the pressure against my clit or my ass. Honestly, I don't want to know.

When he pulls his finger free, the fabric of his suit coat brushes over my ass. I know he's reaching for the plug on the table, and once again, I freeze.

"You can take it, Keira. It's nowhere near as thick as my cock, and barely thicker than my finger. And not only can you take this plug, you're going to love having your ass filled until I tell you to take it out."

I don't want to believe his words, but the dark seduction in them is more than I can handle. His right hand resumes its teasing of my pussy and clit as he presses the end of the plug against my tightest hole.

"You're about to learn what it feels like to have both holes filled at the same time." He slides a finger into my pussy, and the plug fights the resistance of my muscle for a single moment before it slips into my ass and I'm full.

I'm barely starting to adjust to the feeling when Mount's palm connects with my clit with a sharp slap. My back arches as I scream—not in pain, but in mind-bending pleasure.

Mount leans over my prone body, his finger still circling my sensitive clit. "That's your punishment for getting yourself off when I told you not to."

When he says it, I realize I screamed his last name, just like he told me I would. I want to hate myself and him for it, but his hands are too busy. One circles my clit while the other puts pressure on the base of the plug. My thighs, now coated in my own wetness, squeeze together as another orgasm bears down on me. He stills before it bursts over me.

"You don't want to know what the penalty is for taking this out before I tell you to, do you, Keira?"

TWENTY-TWO

Keira

'M A MESS BY THE TIME MOUNT DRAGS THE THONG back up my legs and maneuvers it into place, making sure to press against the base of the plug again, sending aftershocks through me. Literally, figuratively, and any other possible way you can conceive.

He lifts me off his lap as though I weigh nothing and stands me on my feet, keeping a grip on one hip as the hem of the dress falls back into place. As soon as I'm upright, I remember the whole reason for this exercise.

"Shit! I'm going to be late." I bolt toward the door, but Mount's deep voice stops me.

"You have plenty of time. Your meeting doesn't start for another hour."

I swing around and all the heat humming through my body freezes. "You lied to me."

His only answer is a dismissive shrug.

"You—"

He interrupts me before I can curse him. "From now on, every time you call me an asshole, a bastard, or any other slur, or tell me you hate me, I'm going to put you over my knee or bend you over the nearest flat surface. I'll either spank your ass or your pussy, or fuck one of them. No one speaks to me like that without repercussions, and you just got your last free pass."

I swallow the insult that's on my tongue, wondering how in the hell I'm going to manage not to swear at him or tell him I hate him. He makes me so goddamned angry, I can't control my own responses.

No one has ever had that kind of power over me, and I hate that he does.

I square my shoulders and stand as tall as my frame allows. "You can't control everything."

He rises from the chair. "And you've never been more wrong. Get your coat. You wouldn't want to be late for your meeting."

I snatch it off the floor where I dropped it, and shove my arms into it.

"That thing is ugly as hell."

"It's the only one I have, so I guess you have to deal with it." I refuse to look at him.

As I walk toward the door, I feel him stalking close behind me. His suit coat brushes against my arm when he reaches around to open the door, and his heat envelops my body.

When the door swings open, my mouth drops open in shock.

It was unlocked this whole time. I could have run.

Maybe in my dreams. I wouldn't have made it two steps before Mount reached me. And who knows what that punishment would have been.

My ass clenches, too aware of the foreign object inside it.

Scar waits in the hall with the hood. Is it too much to hope he's deaf as well as apparently mute?

"Make sure she gets to the distillery before nine. Pick her up at six. She's not working late this evening because I have plans."

I turn to argue because he's speaking to Scar like I'm not present, but Mount's features might as well be carved from granite. That's when I realize that this is the Mount his employees know. The Mount *everyone* knows. The implacable, cold man whose orders are never questioned or denied. The man who rules with an iron fist and no velvet glove.

When his hard eyes land on me, it's like I'm staring at a different person. I have no doubt this man is every bit as ruthless as his reputation declares.

This isn't the man who carefully surveyed my injured hand last night—before dousing it in fire—but I can't argue that it doesn't hurt today at all because of his actions. This also isn't the man who was just inside that sitting room, making sure I gained as much pleasure from my first experience with anal play as possible.

Which one is the real Mount? Do I even want to know? Does it matter?

The questions stay with me as Scar hands me the hood and silently carries me away. I tell myself I'm imagining it, but I swear I can feel Mount's gaze burn into my back as we leave.

"I don't think we'll have any trouble giving you a little more leeway on your line of credit while you wait for that check to come through, Ms. Kilgore."

Lloyd Bunt delivers his opinion to my chest rather than to my eyes, and I don't know whether I want to curse Mount for leaving my nipples perpetually hard or thank him, because that ridiculous fact might have just bought Seven Sinners a little more time.

I sink back into my chair with a sigh of relief, and the movement shifts the plug in my ass. I paste a smile on my face, not that it matters because Bunt is still staring at my boobs. "I appreciate the consideration. We have several other promising proposals out for bid that will no doubt lead to additional large payments on the line of credit and on the principal of our loan."

Bunt finally raises his gaze to my eyes. "Excellent to hear. We'll look forward to seeing those payments in the near future. And . . . you know, we should probably get another meeting on the calendar as a check-in before I leave. Perhaps next time over dinner?"

My banker is not asking me on a date. That's seriously not happening.

"I can get us a great table at Galatoire's any time."

Yes. Yes, he is. Great.

How do I reply to this delicately? I don't want him reconsidering the deal he just struck with my boobs—*I mean, me.* I scramble for a diplomatic answer.

"I think I'll be burning the midnight oil for some time just to make absolutely sure Seven Sinners stays as profitable as I know it's going to be for a long time to come."

Bunt smiles. "Then how about dinner in the restaurant upstairs? Surely the boss gets to take time to eat in her own establishment?"

He's not going to let me get out of this easily, is he?

"Of course. It's my humble opinion that Odile rivals the best chefs in town."

"Great. Then how about tomorrow night?"

I smile while gritting my teeth. *The man doesn't understand the word* subtle *in the least.* "Let me check with my assistant. She knows my calendar better than I do. I'll get back to you on that."

"Good. I'll expect a call from you tomorrow." He hands me his card. "My cell number is on here as well. Only my favorite clients get this one."

"Wow. Thank you. I don't know what to say," I reply, and it's the absolute truth.

"Just say yes to dinner, Keira. I'd love to get to know you better."

Finally, the excuse I should have been using all along snaps into my brain, and I smile sadly. "In the interest of full disclosure, Lloyd, I'm really still . . . in a grieving period, so friendship is all I'm capable of right now."

His smile reflects his sympathy for all of two seconds. "I absolutely understand. I think we could be *great* friends, Keira. It would further our working relationship too. When I have a vested interest in certain clients, I go above and beyond to make sure their files are kept on my desk, instead of . . ."

He doesn't finish the rest of his sentence, but it's implied. If I agree to dinner, he'll make sure to keep my loan out of workout. Then again, I'm not naive enough to think his expectations would end with dinner.

"I'll be in touch, Keira." He gives me another smarmy smile as he rises from the chair and gathers my loan documents to tuck them in his briefcase. When he finishes, he pauses. "I'm really looking forward to dinner."

To him, it's a foregone conclusion.

I nod as he leaves my office, and can't help but think that his suit hangs on him like a little boy playing dress-up. Nothing like the way Mount's fit him to perfection, accentuating his broad shoulders and narrow waist.

My unruly brain adds *broad shoulders you clawed with your nails* . . . and I shut it down. I shouldn't even be making a comparison between the two men.

And if Mount knew what Bunt suggested . . . I shiver at the thought of what might happen to my banker.

I still wonder if Mount has cameras in my office, and if he does, whether they're wired for sound too. It's a question I should ask, but the man with the granite features that I left this morning isn't one who will give me any answers.

I sit back down at my desk and stack my copies of

the loan documents to return them to their file. Seven Sinners is barely staying in the black. These events have to come through, or I'm going to need a miracle.

Before I can contemplate the topic further, there's a knock on my door and Temperance pokes her head in.

"How'd it go?"

The smile I shoot her way is genuine. "Seven Sinners will live to fight another day. Hopefully many, many days."

"I knew you could do it." Her gaze skims over my dress. "And your outfit is on point, boss. You've stepped it up in the fashion department for these meetings. Smart."

I can't admit that I had nothing to do with these choices, but I suppose I should be grateful they worked in my favor, even if my last two business victories leave a bad taste in my mouth because they feel manipulative.

But I'm not the one manipulating things here, I remind myself.

I don't need to use my boobs to succeed in business, but Mount's point was again hammered home this morning. I have been oblivious to how men looked at me, and now I'm hypersensitive to it.

Another knock sounds on the door. I expect Louis to pop his head in, but it's an unfamiliar face.

"Breakfast delivery for Ms. Kilgore. The receptionist said I should bring it here."

I open my mouth to say that I didn't order any breakfast, but that would raise questions from Temperance I'm not prepared to answer. "Thank you.

Here is fine."

The delivery guy steps inside, and I open my desk drawer to grab some cash for a tip, but he waves it away.

"We're all set. Enjoy."

Temperance turns to watch him walk away. "He was cute. What restaurant is that from? I might need to order some takeout."

"Uh . . ." I stare down at the plain brown bag devoid of any logo. "You know, that new place I've been wanting to try." I snap my fingers like the name is escaping me, frustrated that there's no receipt stapled to the bag with a name. "I swear it'll come to me as soon as you walk out the door."

Temperance eyes me with a strange expression on her face. "Okay. Keep the cute delivery guy to yourself if you want."

"It's not that—"

She holds up both hands. "Hey, if you call dibs, I'm not one to judge."

"No dibs. All yours. I swear. I'm just flustered from the meeting and all the stress leading up to it. And now I have to figure out how to get out of having dinner with Lloyd Bunt."

Her expression swiftly changes to disgust. "He asked you out? During a business meeting? That's just plain unprofessional. Plus, he's . . . ugh." She shudders to drive her opinion home, and I can't disagree with her. Lloyd is the last man I want to have dinner with.

Shouldn't Mount be the last man you want to have dinner with? My logical brain taunts me with the question.

I tell it to shut the hell up as I tear open the brown bag. "I'm going to eat this while it's hot."

Temperance slips out the door. "I'll leave you to it then."

As soon as I sit back down in my chair, the plug shifts in my ass and my nipples pucker against my dress. I try to ignore the sensation, but it's impossible. I've spent the entire morning trying to forget how my day started, and my thong is a lost cause. I remember what Mount said about creaming on his pants, and a shaft of embarrassment stabs into me. I wonder if he changed them, or if—

Stop thinking about him.

That's almost as impossible as forgetting I have a butt plug in my ass.

When I reach inside the bag to discover what I'm having for breakfast, I find a note in familiar handwriting.

Eat. Don't leave the building until you're collected.

"That motherfucker," I whisper to myself.

He can't punish me if he can't hear me call him names.

TWENTY-THREE

Keira

"**G**IRL, ARE YOU CRAZY? YOU KNOW WE CAN'T have lunch in your restaurant together. Things don't work that way," Magnolia argues.

"Stop it. You're one of my oldest friends—"

"And I'm infamous, which I earned all by myself, thank you very much."

I think about the note that told me not to leave, and weigh it against the fact that I need more information if I'm going to win my battle to keep my soul intact during this bargain with Mount. I've already come to terms with the fact that I've lost control of my body.

"But I would really *love* to catch up," I say, and Magnolia picks up on my meaning.

"Yeah, I know. I miss being as close as we used to be. Remember how much fun we had that time we celebrated my GED? We need to do that again real soon. After . . . all this. Then we can catch up like old times.

Still miss those days. When three o'clock meant getting out of school instead of waking up to start working."

Her change of subject throws me for a moment, but then I realize she's speaking in code, like she's also worried someone's listening in to our phone calls.

I swear, I wouldn't put it past him to have my phone tapped.

"Yeah, I know what you mean. I miss those times too. We're due to catch up."

"We'll get to one of these days."

"See you around, Mags."

"Same goes, Ke-ke."

I sneak out the back door of my own building to meet the Uber driver I asked to pick me up at an address a half block away. It's 2:45, which means I'll make it to the location Magnolia alluded to by three. I'm new to this cloak-and-dagger stuff, so I hope like hell I got it right.

When we pull up to the run-down restaurant where you have to order at the counter, I hop out of the car. Magnolia's sporty red Lexus is nowhere in sight. Maybe I'm early?

I push open the restaurant door and look around, but she's not here. I take a booth in the back, slightly out of sight, but if I lean far enough to the right, I can see who walks in the door.

Magnolia's not known for her punctuality, but this time, I was sure she'd be prompt. Unless I misread this whole cloak-and-dagger code-word crap.

Luckily, two minutes later, she rushes in the door. "So sorry, honey. Got stuck in traffic."

"Really? Because that's the excuse every time, and there was hardly any on my way here."

Magnolia rolls her eyes. "Glad you could be so lucky—and that you know me well enough to figure out my code."

I lean forward on the table. "Do you really think he's tapping my phone?" There's no question as to which *he* I'm referring to.

Magnolia mirrors my movement. "Ke-ke, he's tapping your ass, ain't he?"

My butt cheeks clench, thinking of what I removed earlier, when a text from an unknown number came through that only included three words: *Take it out.*

I shift against the torn forest-green vinyl of the booth, not wanting to admit it. Then again, Magnolia doesn't need me to confirm. She just shakes her head like I'm a student not catching on to the most basic of concepts.

"If you think we have more than ten or fifteen minutes before he knows exactly where you are, then you're smoking crack."

"He can't be the big, bad boogeyman you make him out to be," I whisper, only half-certain I'm speaking the truth, because I saw how quickly his entire demeanor changed when we left the room this morning. "No one has that kind of power. Plus, I haven't seen any blood spatters or heard any screaming." Silently I add, *except for my own.*

Magnolia narrows her eyes on me with a shake of her head. "I told you he wouldn't just fuck you, he'd mind-fuck you, and he has."

"But—"

She holds up a hand. "If you need to tell yourself he's not a scary-as-hell, ruthless motherfucker to make you feel okay about the fact that you like the way he fucks you, that's fine. But don't for one second think it's the truth. Because that'll be the biggest lie you ever let yourself believe."

I break her stare, focusing on the chipped red tabletop. My words are nearly inaudible. "Then how can I possibly live with myself knowing what I've let him do to me?" My gaze snaps back up to hers. "I begged him for it." My stomach turns as shame drips from my confession.

Her eyes go hard. "Don't you fucking dare feel ashamed of anything that's happened between you two. I told you, he's not someone you're equipped to deal with. Men like him don't exist in your world. You can't fight the game he's running on you. If he wants a woman, he gets her. Rumor is he fucks them crazy. Literally. The women I told you that he had who disappeared? I heard it's because they lose their goddamned minds over him, and he has to sever the connection *permanently* because those bitches won't let go. Don't you dare think for a second that this is something you could possibly have fought against and won."

A thought flashes through my mind. "Permanently, like he kills them?"

"Don't know. Maybe they're living in houses on

the beach somewhere. Or maybe not. But that's not the point. The point is that all you can do is lock down your head and keep a tight grip on your heart and soul while you let your body enjoy the ride."

"He's already in my head. You said he would be, and he is. When I'm around him, hell, even when I'm not, he's turning me into someone I don't even recognize." In that moment, I'm not sure what scares me more—Mount, or the power he has over me.

"You have to fight it. Keep fighting back against him."

I let loose a harsh laugh. "It's not that easy."

"I'm sure it's not." Again, the Formica becomes fascinating, and Magnolia snaps a finger in front of my face. "We don't have long, so you better spill whatever you've got to say."

I press my lips together until I'm sure they're white and bloodless. "He'll punish me if I fight back."

Her dark eyes go wide, and rage burns within them. "You saying he hurts you? Because I might not survive killing him, but I will go down swinging if he hurts you."

"Not like that," I say quickly, shaking my head. "You know . . . like . . . sexually."

Magnolia reels in her mama-bear instincts a hair and runs her lip over her top teeth. "And he makes you like it."

It's not a question, but I answer anyway. "I can't help it. It's—" I cover my face with both hands. "It's too intense. He has this way of making me so crazy, I want to kill him, and then I lose my goddamned mind." I jerk my head up to stare at the ceiling for the final admission. "I begged him to fuck me last night."

Magnolia's only response is silence until I meet her gaze again. "There are no rules, no right or wrong, and no shame when it comes to what happens between a man and a woman if they're both enjoying it. So, cut yourself some slack. Just because he's into control doesn't make him a monster. Plenty of guys like that shit." She pauses. "But you still have to be smart, girl, and we both know you've got that in the bag."

I'm about to disagree with her, because I feel like an idiot when it comes to all things Mount, but I don't have a chance. The restaurant's door opens and my stomach, already in a precarious position, twists into more intricate knots than even my dad, the former Eagle Scout, could manage.

Scar's footsteps thud against the floor as he comes directly toward our booth, not stopping until he stands a foot from the table.

"I think that's your cue to exit, Ke-ke," Magnolia says.

Scar shoots her a dark look that makes me fear for her safety, and I rise, snapping my fingers in his face like Magnolia did to me a few moments before. When his eyes cut back to me, this time they're widened with surprise. It doesn't take much to assume no one snaps at him.

"Don't you dare take this out on her. And you tell Mount if he does, I will find a way to make sure he regrets ever laying eyes on me."

The surprise in Scar's expression morphs into

something else. I'm not sure if it's him thinking I'm a complete idiot to be threatening Mount, or something entirely different. It almost appears to be an expression resembling respect.

He jerks his head toward the door, and I force myself to maintain the boldness that protecting my friend dredged from deep inside me.

I roll my eyes before looking at Magnolia. "He's never said a single word to me. At this point, I'm pretty sure he never will."

I slide out from the booth and she does the same, nudging Scar aside with her generous hip to wrap me in a hug. I expect her to say she loves me and to stay smart, but instead she whispers in my ear.

"They say Mount cut out his tongue for questioning his orders once. Be safe. But even more important, be smart, Ke-ke." Her words hit me like a sucker punch to the gut as she squeezes and then releases me. "Love you, girl."

"Love you too."

Scar turns toward the door, and I'm pretty sure if he could talk, he would say, "Follow me, and no more bullshit."

My trepidation grows with every step I take away from Magnolia and toward the car that will deliver me back to Mount. I disobeyed his direct orders, and I have no doubt I'm going to pay for it.

Scar opens the back door of the sedan and I slide inside. It's pointless to fight, like Magnolia said. All I can do is be smart and reinforce my defense with steel and attitude.

The hood is on the backseat. I want to toss it in Scar's face, but what will that earn me? Another punishment? Probably.

He starts the car but doesn't put it into drive. It takes me several seconds before I meet his gaze in the rearview mirror and get the message loud and clear. He's not moving until I put it on.

"You're an asshole too, in case you were wondering."

I'm not saying it directly to Mount, so I consider it a loophole.

I shove the hood aside. "I'm not going back to him yet either. He said six o'clock, and I still have work to do. Take me to the distillery."

Scar's expression changes into one of shock at my demands. When he shifts the car into drive and pulls out of the parking lot, I'm not sure which way he'll go.

Much to my surprise, he takes me back to work. I tell myself it's a victory, but inside, I know I'm just delaying the punishment that's sure to come later.

TWENTY-FOUR

Keira

WHEN I'M RETURNED TO MY CAGE THAT EVENING by Scar, there's a note on the bathroom mirror I can't miss.

Shower.
You have one hour to be dressed and ready.

I'm smart enough to know when to push and when to yield—a little. After my defiance this afternoon, I decide there's no harm in following the instructions.

After a quick shower, I hurry to get ready in the allotted time. I'm not high maintenance, but it takes forever to dry my hair. I don't have a clue how much time has passed because Scar didn't bring my purse, so I rush through everything I can. I duck into the closet and find a white dress hanging up that's similar in style to the black one I wore earlier. As I slide it on, I can't help but feel like I'm about to become a sacrificial offering.

I'm waiting in the sitting room when Scar arrives, hood in hand again.

At least I made it within the allotted time.

Scar carries me up and down stairs, around twists and turns, and there's no doubt in my mind I'm being delivered to Mount to face the consequences of my actions this afternoon. Magnolia's warnings sweep through my mind again, and I tell myself it was worth it.

When Scar finally places me on my feet, I rip the hood off, instantly on guard.

This is a new room for me. Everything about it exudes power with zero subtlety, including the massive desk that Mount sits behind and the monitors in front of him that slide out of sight, disappearing into hidden compartments.

He looks over my shoulder, rather than at me, and gives Scar a nod. There's a whooshing noise behind me and then silence.

Alone again and completely at his mercy. Or am I?

Mount opens his mouth to speak, but I cut him off before he can start. A good offense is the best defense, right?

"So, now you're tracking my every movement? Sending your henchman to retrieve me the second I step out of line? I told you, you don't get to fuck with every aspect of my life, and I meant it."

The darkness that's almost always present in his expression deepens. "I can't decide if you're stupid or just bold to defy me the way you do."

"So, what are you going to do? Kill me?" Even as the question comes out of my mouth, I regret offering up the idea.

Mount's dark eyes narrow but a chilling smile spreads across his face. "No, but I'm going to make sure you think long and fucking hard about ever disobeying me again."

"You—"

He lifts his chin as if daring me to continue with whatever insult I'm going to hurl at him, and I snap my mouth shut, my teeth closing over my lip to keep it in.

"Come here."

I swallow, because rounding that desk is the last thing I want to do right now, but something in his expression tells me disobedience would be a very bad idea.

My heels, ones that I assume he chose himself, click on the hardwood as I come around the desk toward him. I only make it halfway before Mount shoves out of his heavy leather chair and stops me by gripping me around the waist and lifting me onto his empty desk.

Did he plan this in advance? The trepidation I felt in the restaurant is nothing compared to what's charging through my veins now.

"What are you going to do?"

"Don't make me gag you too."

Too?

His big hand lands between my breasts, and he presses me down until I'm spread flat across the desk, my knees bending over the side. My heels drop off my feet, one at a time, and hit the floor.

"Mount—" True panic comes through when I say his name.

"Do you trust me, Keira?"

He's asked me the question before, and the answer hasn't changed.

"No."

A wolfish grin replaces his expression. "Probably smart."

He crouches between my legs, and I expect to feel cool air hit my skin when he flips up my skirt, but instead he latches something soft around my ankle, locking it to the leg of the desk.

"What the hell—"

Before I can react, the other ankle is subjected to the same treatment, but on the opposite side, leaving my legs spread wide and vulnerable. I jerk against the bonds, but they're just as unyielding as the man before me.

"Don't."

My movement halts at his command.

"See, you can follow orders. And for that, I won't cuff your hands."

His thumbs start at my ankles, just above the buckles, and slide up the inside of my legs until they reach my thighs. He fans out his fingers as they curl around each of my legs, pushing my skirt up inch by inch until my thong is bared to his view.

"Are you scared, Keira?"

Part of me is fucking petrified, but the other part, the part that's clearly insane, is responsible for the slickness already gathering between my legs because of the bondage. Something I'd only tried once before, but I push the thought from my mind. I don't want to remember that crazy Mardi Gras night now because of all the disappointments that came after.

Mount's palms stop with one thumb poised just over my center, and I realize he's waiting for an answer.

"Yes." I force the word from between my lips, and his smile turns victorious.

"You should be. But you're also a little liar." He swipes his thumb down the material of my thong that's becoming more soaked with each moment that passes. "You're already wet for me. You like this. Being at my mercy. Not sure what I'm going to do to you. I could finger you, eat your sweet cunt, or fuck you. Or I could do all three."

My thighs attempt to clench together, but the bonds keep my ankles locked down. Mount doesn't miss the movement of my flexing muscles, though.

"You're a dirty fucking girl, Keira. But I've always known that about you."

"How?" The demand comes out on a wavering breath.

Instead of an answer, he uses his other hand to snap the lace of the thong, tearing it free.

"I swore to myself I wouldn't taste this pussy, wouldn't give you the pleasure until I buried my cock in your mouth, but you've got me breaking more than one of my rules tonight."

A shudder rolls over my body as his nose drags along my inner thigh. He breathes in my scent, then closes his mouth over my center and begins to devour me. He teases my entrance with a finger, my wetness growing with each movement before he pushes it inside, sucking hard on my clit at the same time. He changes his plan of attack to some kind of unholy *make Keira come instantly* play that produces a shock wave of pleasure. My back lifts off the desk as I reach for his hair, and I'm not certain whether I want to yank him away or hold him between my legs so I can experience the intense sensation over and over.

As soon as my fingers bury in his hair, he yanks his face away, shaking his head.

"You just can't follow orders."

He rises to his feet and comes around the desk, then reaches for my hands.

"What—"

"You'll see."

He wraps my wrists in cushion-lined leather cuffs connected by an intricate chain. Mount pushes my spine back down to the surface of his desk and guides my bound hands over my head, clipping them to a hook somewhere below.

He surveys my body like it's a feast spread out on his desk, waiting to be devoured.

The white dress now makes sense. I definitely feel like a sacrificial offering.

"Now I can eat that cunt in peace, and you can't stop me."

"If this is the part where you torture me with orgasms, I'm okay with that."

As soon as the admission is out, part of me wants

to snatch it back, but something about it also fills me with power. Like on some level, I'm *allowing* Mount this privilege. Maybe my mind is well and truly fucked, because the smile that crosses his face, smug yet secretive, only makes me want him to return to his interrupted task faster.

He shakes his head slowly from side to side like he doesn't know what to make of me, and that reinforces the shreds of power I'm grappling to hold on to.

When he crouches between my legs again, circling my clit with one thick fingertip, I writhe, bucking my hips up to increase the pressure, determined to control the situation as much as I can from my position. I may be bound, but I don't feel helpless anymore.

Mount sucks my clit between his teeth and bites down just hard enough to send a jolt of desire laced with a hint of pain through my body.

When he releases his teeth, a slight sting remains, but it's not pain. It's . . . more complicated than that. If he keeps doing it, I'm going to come in the next sixty seconds.

He tongues my entrance before licking up to my clit and nipping it again, and I moan, my head thrashing from side to side. Protests fall from my lips as his mouth recedes and he circles my clit with a fingertip again.

"You love that. The bite of pain with your pleasure. The pressure on your clit constantly taking you to the edge. What if I could keep you on that edge all the time? Ready to come at a moment's notice?"

I swallow, wondering where his diabolical mind is

going. "What are you talking about?"

"An experiment." He reaches around the side of the desk and pulls out a package. I lift my head as much as I can with my arms in their bound position to see what he's doing. I see a flash of silver.

"What is that?"

"You'll see. Or feel, rather."

Cold metal drags across my heated center, and I know exactly what he has—some kind of clamp.

"Let's see how you like this." He closes it lightly over my swollen clit, sending my spine arching off the desk again.

As quickly as the pressure came, it dissipates.

I want it back. Magnolia told me there's no shame if we're both willing, and as messed up as this is, I want more of what he's giving me.

"I could make you wear a clamp twenty-four hours a day to remind you not to disobey, but that's not safe or healthy."

Those are the last words I expect to hear come out of his mouth, and I have no response. But when he stands and the pressure returns again, I'm edging toward an orgasm. He lets off once more.

"But there is another option, one I think you'd fucking love. And I know I will."

I don't know what he's talking about, but I'm so close to the edge, I'm mindless with need. "Please—"

"You want to come?"

"Yes!"

"Then tell me you'll pierce that sweet little hood so the jewelry rubs your clit with your every movement, keeping you wet and ready for me."

His words penetrate the lust-filled haze in my head, dragging me back to reality.

"What?"

"A hood piercing. It'll heighten your every sensation. Some women even claim it causes spontaneous orgasms."

My mouth falls open, but not because of shock like he probably assumes.

How does he infiltrate my thoughts?

I've thought about getting my hood pierced for years, and almost did before I met Brett. I brought it up once to him, but he dismissed it as a stupid idea.

That didn't stop me from wanting it, though, and wondering what it would be like. My hips shift from side to side as Mount studies me like he's reading my every reaction and expression.

"You've already had it done before?" This is actually a question, one of the few he's truly asked me.

I shake my head. "No."

"But you wanted to do it."

I bite down on my lip, not wanting to actually admit it.

Mount doesn't need to hear my confession. He reads it on my face.

"You're getting it pierced tonight."

This time, my mouth drops open in shock. "What?"

"I swore I'd keep this pussy to myself, but I want you pierced with the jewelry I choose. An emerald. Every time I spread your legs, I want to see it flash at me the same way your eyes do."

His tongue circles my clit, teasing and testing before nipping and tugging. My hips press up against his mouth, increasing the pressure, but he backs off again.

"Tell me you want it."

"I want to come," I say instead.

"Not until you admit you want that piercing. That you want to feel it between your legs, and that every time you move, you'll think of me, even without your ass or pussy filled."

His finger lazily circles my entrance, pushing in and out to the first knuckle, teasing me until I want to scream. I manage to keep my silence for another ninety seconds. I count them in my head, and I can't hold back any longer.

"Just let me come."

His finger plunges inside me, fucking me now.

"Not until you tell me you want it. I can see it in your face, but I need to hear it from those fuckable lips."

At this point, I'm ready to agree to nearly anything this manipulative son of a bitch demands, but the fact that it's something I've secretly wanted for years? What do I have to lose?

"Fine! Yes! I want it. Now, let me come."

True to his word, Mount devours me again, his lips, teeth, tongue, and fingers getting me off in record time. As soon as the orgasm shimmers through my body like some kind of voodoo magic, he stands and flips my skirt down.

"Don't ever say I never gave you anything you asked for."

He pulls his phone from his pocket and taps on

the screen. He starts to speak as he walks away from where I'm still bound to the desk.

"I need a piercer. Tonight. Female." Mount pauses. "Yeah, she'll do. Make sure she knows what happens if she talks. Get her here in fifteen minutes with her equipment and gold-and-emerald jewelry." Another pause. "Make it happen." He ends the call.

The reality of what I've agreed to crashes into me. "We're really doing this? Now? Tonight?"

Mount turns around to face me. "You think I'm going to give you a chance for second thoughts? You want it. I'm willing to bet you've wanted it for years." He tilts his head to the side, as though trying to read my mind. "Are you capable of telling the truth, or are you going to lie to me again?"

His challenge forces my honesty. "I've thought about it."

"Why didn't you do it? You go after everything else you want."

I don't answer, but he makes an assumption that's probably accurate.

"Ah. Well now, you don't have that problem any-more. I think it's hot as fuck, and I can't wait to see you pierced."

I tug at my bindings. "Are you . . . are you going to leave me like this when she comes?" I heard him re-quest a female, and was actually thankful for that.

"Will you behave if I let you free?"

"I hate that word," I tell him. "You make me sound like a child."

He lowers to a crouch and reaches for the buckle

on one of my ankles before rephrasing his question. "Are you going to make me regret not gagging you and keeping you bound? Because the consequences of your actions over the next hour will affect not only you, but someone else's life."

I let several hammering heartbeats pass before I nod. "You have nothing to worry about."

At that reply, he huffs out a laugh and unbuckles that ankle and then the other before moving to free my wrists.

"Why is that funny?"

"Someday, I might tell you."

When my legs are free, I slide them shut, well aware I'm going to have to spread them again, but this time for a stranger with a needle. I'm finally going to get the naughty piercing I've wanted since college but was never brave enough to actually get.

Is that what Mount's doing? Pushing me outside my comfort zone?

Undoubtedly.

And I like it.

Within fifteen minutes, there's a knock at the door and Mount calls out, "Enter."

The bookcase slides open, and Scar escorts in a woman who *isn't* a stranger.

"Delilah?"

Her eyes widen beneath her bright blue bangs. "Holy shit. I didn't see that coming."

"And you'll keep your mouth shut about it," Mount says to her, his tone threatening.

Delilah looks from me to him, her posture

stiffening. "I'm only doing this if she's willing. If this is something you're trying to force on her, you'll have to find someone else."

Mount's expression hardens to granite like it did this morning, and I wonder if I'm the only person who sees the other side of him. What Magnolia told me this afternoon makes me think that's the case, and I'm not sure what to do with that knowledge yet.

"Do you want to live until morning?" Mount asks Delilah, and she bites down on her lip.

There's no way I'm going to let him hurt her. For the first time, I modulate my tone before I speak to him, in consideration of my recent discovery that he *isn't* the same man when there's someone else in the room.

"She's a friend. It's okay." I reach out a hand and catch the arm of his suit jacket to give it the slightest tug.

Mount drops his gaze to where I'm touching him before dragging it up to my face with a new intensity.

"She won't say anything," I say quietly.

The weight of his silence nearly crushes us all. Finally, he speaks. "Then we have no issue."

When I release my hold on his arm, he flexes his fingers before balling them into a fist. He uncurls them a second later and shoves his hands into the pockets of his suit pants.

I look across the room to where Delilah stands. Her posture is tense, as if she's poised to run for the exit, and I can't say I blame her. The Mount she's subjected to is the ruthless bastard everyone else knows.

"I want to do this," I tell her.

"You're sure?"

"Yes."

"Have you been drinking?" she asks.

"No more questions." Mount snaps out his response.

Delilah glances up at him, only willing to meet his gaze for the barest moment before looking back to me. "It's important to know for bleeding issues."

I answer her. "I'm completely sober."

She gives me a look that says, *You might be sober but something is totally fucked up about this situation.*

Delilah's not wrong about that.

"Okay, then let's do this," she says with a nod, and Scar hands her the toolbox I didn't notice he was holding until just now. As soon as he hands it off, he leaves the room.

Within a few moments, I'm again lying back on Mount's desk, this time of my own volition. Either that or I'm losing my fucking mind. It could be either at this point, honestly.

Delilah has me sanitized, prepped, and ready a few minutes later, and Mount stands beside the desk, next to me.

When I catch sight of the long, thick needle that's going to push through a *very* sensitive part of my anatomy, the jewelry threaded on one end, gold with an emerald crystal as requested, I start to second-guess my decision.

"Just take a few deep breaths in and out for me," Delilah tells me, like we're sitting in Voodoo Ink and this isn't some crazy house call. "It's not nearly as bad as what you're imagining. I promise."

I breathe as she instructed, but I'm still freaking out inside.

"Okay," Delilah says. "I'm going to tell you to take a deep breath in through your nose and then blow it out through your mouth, and we'll be done before you know it. Deep breath in," she orders, and my hand snakes out beside me, clamping around Mount's fingers as I comply. "Now, blow it out."

I grip his hand as I do it, and he squeezes back.

The sting is there and gone in an instant.

"And you're almost done." Delilah's tone is congratulatory. "Just let me unscrew this and get the end of the jewelry tightened down, and you'll be good to go."

I loosen my hold on Mount's hand, but he doesn't let go. I tell myself it's because my lungs are still heaving at a rate likely to cause hyperventilation.

After a few more efficient movements, Delilah stands and snaps off her latex gloves. Mount drops my hand instantly.

"You're all set. I can leave after-care instructions for you. But one thing . . ." Her gaze darts to Mount for a second before returning to me. "You're going to want to be gentle with it for a few days. It'll be healed within a week, but . . . take it easy for a couple days. You'll know if you overdo it. And you also know where to find me if you have any issues or questions."

I flip my skirt down and close my legs. "Thank you. You're pretty good at that."

Delilah shrugs. "Somehow, I always get stuck doing the piercings, but this is a pretty easy one. So much less painful than the nipples."

My gaze shifts to Mount's, and I hope he's not getting any ideas. I'm a big fan of my nipples exactly the way they are.

"No, thank you," I say with emphasis. "I'm not piercing those."

"Good." She looks at the panel that conceals the hidden door where she entered. "Now, how the hell do I get out of this place?"

TWENTY-FIVE

Keira

AFTER DELILAH LEAVES, MOUNT ESCORTS ME BACK to my room, and it's the first time I'm allowed to walk through the maze of hidden passageways and stairs with my sight intact. However, most of my attention is focused on the new sensitivity between my legs. With each step, my clit seems to swell and my body heats.

Spontaneous orgasms aren't really possible, right?

I push the thought away and think of something else. Like the fact that something shifted in Mount's office as Delilah pierced me.

For the first time ever, I touched him voluntarily, and I know Mount didn't miss that fact. Maybe that's why I'm being granted the privilege of being able to see where my room lies in relation to what I assume is Mount's inner sanctum.

It doesn't take me long before I realize this isn't one building, it's multiple buildings connected by corridors and stairs, built at least a hundred years before I was born. My best guess? We're somewhere in the French Quarter, and when we walk through an open courtyard, I can hear the sound of revelry not far away.

Which means the building or buildings are most likely soundproof. Good to know. I also spy a wrought-iron gate at the back of the courtyard and catch a glimpse of taillights as a car drives by on either a street or alley.

"I won't fuck you tonight, unless you think your ass is ready after spending the morning wearing that plug."

The thought of the car and gate vanishes from my head as I jerk my gaze up to Mount's.

"Uh, that would be a hard no, chief."

A rough chuckle leaves his lips as he leads me into another building, and I'm guessing this one is where my suite is housed. We climb two more sets of stairs before we reach the internal set of rooms.

Mount opens the door and gestures for me to enter before following me inside. "Then we better step up your training. Use the facilities if you need them, then I want you bent over the end of the bed, naked and waiting."

"What?" I sound shocked because tonight has already been overwhelming enough.

"How else am I gonna stretch your ass to fit my cock if you don't take a thicker plug?"

"It's only been one day! This is a process. It should take weeks."

He reaches down and grasps the thick shaft pressing against his suit pants. "You've got three days, and I'm being generous. Now, go."

His tone, softer than what it was in the room with Delilah present, still invites no argument. And here I thought something had changed. Apparently, I was wrong.

I take care of my business in the bathroom, sucking in a breath as my new jewelry connects with my clit, sending a jolt of pleasure through me.

Oh, good God. Maybe that spontaneous orgasms thing is true? I could be okay with that.

I walk out of the bathroom to find Mount standing with another box in one hand and lube in the other.

"The longer you wait, the less you're going to enjoy this."

I bite my lip because I'm already turned on because of the new piercing, but also what came before. I bend over the end of the bed, for the first time realizing it's the perfect height for him to fuck me like this.

I wonder if that's intentional?

"Good girl. Lift your skirt and show me that ripe peach of an ass."

His dirty words are my undoing every time.

I comply, because I can't not. It doesn't make sense, but that's how I feel as I squirm on the bed, bumping the new jewelry, sending jolts of pleasure zinging out from my clit through the rest of me.

"Fuck, I don't know what turns me on more. When you fight me or when you obey." His palm strokes my ass almost reverently. "As much as I want to fuck you right now, I won't. But I'm sure as hell not waiting a week for that pussy." A cold drizzle of lube hits my crack, and Mount spreads it around my hole.

Now that I know what's coming, I try not to tense. I can't say that I didn't enjoy this earlier today, even when I wanted to hate it.

As he rims the pucker with lube, he presses against it with a finger until it gives way with less resistance. "No longer completely virgin territory, but it won't be official until my cock is buried inside this tight hole." His lubed finger slides inside to the second knuckle, and I fight the urge to press back against it. "After this plug, you'll take two fingers and I'll stretch you more. Eventually I'm going to fit, and you're going to fucking love it."

I believe him, and that scares me more than any butt plug ever could.

He removes his finger and lubes up the plug, pressing the tip against me. "Press your pussy against the bed and then push out as I slide it in. This one's thicker, but still not as big as my cock."

I do as he says, the pressure on my new jewelry unleashing a torrent of sparks from my clit as he presses the plug inside, fucking me slowly with it.

"My little hellion is finally acting like a good girl. Finally taking what I give you. Letting me fuck your ass. Piercing your clit. Bending you over my lap."

His words throw me over the edge into orgasm with a wail. My own cries almost drown out his words, but I still catch them.

"Sweet fucking Christ, I want you so goddamned bad right now, but—" He cuts off his own words and seats the plug with a final push.

As I release a breathy moan, Mount flips down the

skirt of my dress, turns, and is at the bedroom door before I stand up.

All I catch is the sight of his perfectly tailored suit coat stretching across his broad shoulders as he strides away. But he doesn't make his usual silent exit.

This time, the door slams, and I'm left more confused than I've been yet.

A new tingle pulses between my legs, but it's not my *accessories* causing the confusion. No, that's due to one very specific man who I don't have the urge to curse to the devil for the first time since this all began.

TWENTY-SIX

Keira

MOUNT ISN'T WAITING IN MY ROOM THE NEXT morning like a part of me hopes.

I remove the plug myself, but there isn't another box waiting for me. There is, however, another outfit. This time it's a white blouse and high-waisted black pleated skirt with a gold chain belt. The bra is lacy and white and appears that it might be marginally effective at shielding nipples today, because the piercing is rendering me more sensitive than normal. There are matching panties, which brush against the jewelry constantly, driving me crazy in the best way possible. The pumps are black patent leather and higher than anything I've ever worn. They also feature the famous red soles I've always coveted but could never afford. When I slide my feet into them, I can't help but survey my appearance in the full-length closet mirror.

I look good. Even I can admit that.

I eat the breakfast that's waiting in the sitting room,

but Mount still doesn't appear. I wait for Scar to collect me, and after last night and being escorted back to my room without the hood, I'm hoping it's gone for good.

Not so.

For some reason, it seems more insulting than it did before, if that's even possible.

As I walk in the door to the distillery, I vow to focus on business all day, and nothing else.

I'm marginally successful. I wait for another text from the unknown number.

Nothing.

No food deliveries. No notes. Complete silence, almost like Mount has disappeared from my life, leaving a hood piercing as my only souvenir.

This is a good thing, I tell myself, even as I begin to worry that something is massively wrong. I help Temperance nail down the final details of the football event and check almost every item off my to-do list, a task that has been impossible to accomplish for months.

"You're in beast mode today, boss. Nice work."

I shoot my assistant a smile as she leaves my office. "I only work in beast mode. Ever."

When I'm finishing up a final task and ready to wrap it up for the day, Temperance bursts into my office without knocking.

"Holy shit. Have you seen the news?"

"No. What happened? Someone get traded?"

Her face, already pale, loses its remaining color. "No. They found Lloyd Bunt's body this afternoon."

Everything in me goes still except the blood

pounding at my temples and whooshing through my ears. "What did you say?"

"Lloyd Bunt. He's dead. They're saying it was suicide, or maybe murder. They haven't been able to rule either out. But he wasn't alone."

I curl my fingers around the arms of my desk chair. "Who was he with?"

"A hooker. There's speculation that her cause of death was autoerotic asphyxiation."

Lloyd Bunt. Murder. Or suicide. With a dead hooker. The facts slam through my brain like cars in a head-on collision.

"That's awful." My voice shakes, and I truly mean it. Just a few minutes ago, when I was putting the loan docs back in the filing cabinet where they belong, I was counting myself lucky that he hasn't contacted me today.

Now I know why.

Or who.

"I have to go." I grab my purse and my trench coat and rush past Temperance, bolting out of my office.

Scar is waiting out front with the car. I yank the back door open, not waiting for him to come around and get it for me.

"Take me to him," I demand.

Scar meets my gaze in the rearview mirror and nods before tossing the hood at me.

I don't complain as I pull it on, because I need to see Mount *right now*. We take the usual—and what I assume is a ridiculously inefficient—route to return, and I don't fight as Scar carries me to my sitting room.

My jail cell.

That I only get to leave on work release.

Everything about this feels completely and totally wrong, if what I suspect is true.

Mount isn't just ruthless. He's a psychopath.

I pace the room, working myself up more and more until he finally arrives what feels like an eternity later.

I don't wait for him to speak before I fire my question at him. "Did you do it?"

His expression, already blank, doesn't change. "Do what?"

"Did you kill him?"

Mount raises that arrogant fucking eyebrow. "You're going to have to be more specific."

"Lloyd Bunt. My banker."

"The one who attempted to begin forcing you into a sexual relationship yesterday?" Mount asks.

My stomach drops to the floor. *I can't be responsible for Lloyd's death. I can't be*, I tell myself.

To Mount, I give a different reply. "That's not what it was. He only wanted dinner. A date."

"And he would've kept pushing for more. Threatening your precious distillery until he got exactly what he wanted. To fuck you." Mount's declaration is harsh, and bile rises in my throat.

"And how is that any different from what *you* did?" I fling the accusation at him like a knife, and his blank expression disappears as his dark gaze flares.

"I was fucking honest about what I wanted—you in trade for the debt. No bullshit. Lloyd Bunt couldn't wipe your debt away. He didn't have a single fucking

226

shred of real power."

"But—" I start to argue, but Mount interrupts.

"And there's another important difference."

"What?"

"You didn't want him."

My shoulders stiffen. "And you think I wanted you?"

"I know you did, whether or not you'll admit it to yourself."

"You arrogant asshole—" When Mount steps forward, I hold out one hand like I could possibly stop him. "Don't you dare fucking touch me right now. Or ever again."

My hand may not have the desired effect, but my words stop him cold. And when I say cold, I mean *frigid.*

Mount's features harden into the granite mask he never uses on me as he turns to walk away.

"You killed him, didn't you? And her!"

Once more, Mount ignores my question and slams the door on his way out.

TWENTY-SEVEN

Keira

As soon as the door is closed, I run to grab my purse and my phone. I have zero cell service and no Internet connection, both of which must be controlled by Mount. I wait about two minutes before I head for the door and try the knob.

It turns freely.

In his fury, the all-powerful Mount forgot the most important thing—you can't keep an unwilling prisoner in an unlocked cell.

I dash into the hallway, retracing the path we used last night until I reach the courtyard. The hallways are silent and empty, and I don't give a damn if the cameras catch me. My goal is to be out of the gate and gone before he can reach me.

I don't know if it's the good Lord smiling down on me or a twist of fate finally working in my favor, but the courtyard gate is secured with a double dead bolt from the inside and not a key.

As soon as I hit the cracked sidewalk of a familiar block of the French Quarter, I take my first breath of freedom, but I know I can't waste any time appreciating it. I sprint down the street to one where I know there will be cabs waiting, expecting Mount or Scar to yank me back into the shadows at any moment.

But they don't.

Probably too busy covering up a double homicide.

I slide into the first cab that stops and give the driver the address to my apartment. I know it sounds stupid, but I'm hoping Mount will assume I'm too smart to go there, which will buy me some time. Maybe.

The cabdriver fights traffic while I grasp my apartment keys in my purse until the sharp metal edges make my eyes sting with tears. I have to keep it together, even though I feel like everything is splintering out of control. I can't risk going to the police because I have no idea who is on Mount's payroll. More than one, I would bet on that.

Nothing is what it seems. Or maybe everything is *exactly* as it seems. Mount is the villain here. He manipulated me, and I fell under his spell. End of story.

As soon as we reach my block, I toss some cash at the cabbie and run up the sidewalk to the door. Again, I'm expecting to be captured at any moment, and God knows what they'll do to me now. I have nothing to lose and everything to gain by finding the gun I keep locked in my nightstand drawer. After I have some way to protect myself, I'll find a cop who isn't on Mount's payroll.

As soon as I step into my apartment, I scan every surface in the open kitchen and living room area. It doesn't look like anyone has been here.

I race to the bedroom, intent on getting the gun and as many rounds as I have left in the box of ammo. I have to be ready because I know he'll come for me.

When I rush for the nightstand drawer, there's a box on the bed that brings me to a halt. A black one. The same type that carried each of the sex toys Mount used on me.

I grab it off my bed and fling it at the wall, not caring about the dent it will leave. I expect a vibrator or a butt plug to fall to the floor, but neither do.

What looks like a pair of underwear and a piece of paper flutter to the floor.

What the hell?

Looking over my shoulder out of instinct, I slowly cross the room and crouch down to retrieve them.

I expect the bold handwriting I've come to know as Mount's, but the curving feminine letters were written by my own hand.

I remember writing the note all too vividly.

Meet me at Bal Masqué in the back alcove at midnight. Don't say anything. Just take me.

Reading the familiar words drops me to my knees. I grab black fabric. It's a thong I bought specifically to match the jeweled bra I wore under my gown for Bal Masqué.

It was just after Brett and I met and we were still in

the sexy, flirtatious phase, which quickly turned into a whirlwind courtship. We got married the next day, in large part because of the events of that night.

How could Mount have these?

A chill snakes down my spine as my memory of that night returns.

Seven Months Earlier

I couldn't believe I was doing this, but God, it finally felt good to take control and demand what I wanted. What I needed. This was the test, the true test to find out if Brett could be the man who would give me what I'd been missing my whole life.

I slipped into the dark alcove, away from the dancing, hoping he'd gotten the note. If not, I'd be going home disappointed and sexually frustrated.

Basically, my normal state in life, it seemed, especially lately.

I looked down at the watch I wore, even though it didn't go with my outfit, because I wanted to make sure I didn't miss the midnight deadline.

I needed a man who wasn't afraid to take charge, and I didn't know how I could be any clearer about what I needed other than to spell it out like I did in my note. This was make or break for Brett and me, as far as I was concerned.

Both hands of my watch landed on the twelve, and I turned toward the wall in the hidden alcove that was known for trysts. Honestly, I was lucky to find it empty. Well, not lucky. As soon as people saw me here for the last half hour, they moved off to find another likely location.

I wanted what they were having.

Why was that so much to ask for?

Heavy footsteps sounded on the marble floor behind me and I stilled, keeping my face toward the wall. My nipples peaked and I clenched my thighs together in anticipation. I was already wet and ready, since I'd been thinking about how incredible this night could be.

A hand closed over my bare shoulder, and when I tried to spin around, his other hand gripped me by the waist, pushing me toward the wall before binding my hands with something soft. Silk?

Thank you, Lord!

He didn't say anything, and the unique scent of citrus mingled with spice and woodsy notes stole over me, kicking up my desire another notch. The hand on my waist gripped the skirt of my long ball gown and yanked it up until cool air rushed over my thong-clad behind. I wondered if he could see the sparkling crystals winking in the dim light. It was probably dumb to buy special lingerie for this occasion, but I was ever the optimist.

He groaned as he cupped my ass and squeezed hard, no hesitation in his touch. Only the dominance I needed.

Again, I tried to turn my head but he wouldn't let me, wrapping a hand around my throat and pulling me back against him as his decadent scent washed over me.

The gesture said it all. He was in control and I was at his mercy, which was exactly what I wanted.

Releasing my throat, he wrapped my hair in his hand and forced me to bend forward a few more inches.

One foot nudged mine, and I spread my legs for him willingly.

"Please." The plea came out as a moan, and he met it with a deep growl.

He released my hair to slide his hand between my legs. My thong was soaked. My desire dripped down my thighs, but I wasn't ashamed of it. His deep groan told me he thought it was sexy as hell.

He tucked a finger under the back strap of the thong and followed it down to the part that was drenched with my slickness. That's when he truly turned into the barbarian I'd been hoping he would be.

His grip went to the top band and he shredded the delicate lace, tearing it from my hips. He wasted no time finding my clit and teasing it with slow circles before plunging a thick finger inside me.

"Ahhhh." When he paused at my breathy moan, I urged him on. "No. Don't stop. Please. You have to fuck me. I swear I'll die if I don't have you inside me right now."

A growl of satisfaction met my ears and he finger-fucked me, alternating with teasing my clit until my orgasm burst through me. His hand disappeared as pleasure swamped me, but only for a moment. The music from the ball faded away as I focused on the sounds right behind. A zipper. The crinkle of foil as he tore open a condom.

Thank God one of us was thinking, because I'd lost all normal brain function at this point.

With one hand, he pinned the skirt of my dress to my back and guided his cock to my entrance with the other. As soon as he fit it against my slick heat, he plunged forward, burying himself with a single thrust.

I sucked in a ragged breath as his thickness stretched me decadently, almost to the point of pain, but all I felt was pleasure. My moans turned into cries, and he released his hold on my dress and covered my mouth with his hand while he fucked into me over and over, harder and deeper with each thrust. A scream threatened to leave my lips, and my only choice was to dig my teeth into the palm covering my mouth, not even caring that I might leave marks. His mouth dropped to the curve where my shoulder met my neck, and his teeth scraped across my skin before sucking hard.

My orgasm shattered inside me as he tore his mouth away, but he didn't stop his movements. He dropped his hand from my mouth and released mine from their bondage, bringing one to my lips to silence myself so he could continue to work my clit and fuck me harder and deeper at the same time.

I didn't do nearly as good a job at covering the sound of my orgasm as he did. I was pretty sure the entire ballroom heard me yell, "Yes! God, yes!" as another one ripped through me.

My inner muscles clamped down on his thick cock as it pulsed inside me, his orgasm filling me with a sense of power.

I did that.

And it was fucking incredible.

He pulled out of me and I lost my balance, stumbling to the side as I tried to right my skirt. He steadied me with a hand on my waist before crouching down. I leaned against the wall, still attempting to catch my breath. The grin on my face widened as I realized I'd finally found the one. The man who could give me all the things I needed.

But when I turned around, he was gone.

Disappointment slammed into me, but then I realized he was just following through with my request. *Say nothing. Just take me.*

And he did.

Spectacularly.

As I took a step to leave the alcove, I remembered my torn panties. There was definitely no way I wanted to leave those lying around for someone to find and speculate as to their ownership. I searched the marble floor almost blindly, but found nothing.

Well, hell. It wasn't like I could wear them again anyway.

I left the ballroom with the biggest smile on my face that I'd had in years, and feeling like the queen of this masquerade.

Tomorrow, I was going to talk Brett into eloping.

Present day

That scent. The same fucking scent that hung in my office after Mount delivered his ultimatum. And those hands. The way he touched me.

God, I replayed that scene from the masquerade in my head so many times to get myself off after Brett would roll over, satisfied after a few pumps, and leave me wondering what the hell happened to the man who took me like he owned me that night.

All the similarities . . . His groans. His growls. The way he took without apology. The way he fucked me the way I needed to be fucked.

I already knew my marriage was based on a web of lies, but didn't realize that the very foundation of my decision to marry Brett was based on deception too.

There's no doubt in my mind that somehow, some way, Mount found that note and decided to meet me that night. How he knew who I was or why he decided to do it, I have no idea.

But what does that change?

Nothing.

After the last few days, I know he can play my body better than any man I've ever met—save one. The only competition he had was himself.

That fucking bastard.

I wanted it. That night at the masquerade and every single time he touched me. *I begged him.*

And that fact just makes me hate him more.

I could kill him.

But I remember the cold mask that settled over

his features as I accused him of murder tonight, and I know I have to protect myself.

I flip on the nightstand lamp, and a stack of documents that wasn't there before greets me.

My loan from the bank. The promissory note is stamped PAID IN FULL with yesterday's date. The line of credit. The term note. All of it. Almost two million dollars' worth of debt, all paid in full. I flip through the documents, on the verge of losing my mind as my stomach twists into knots.

Mount did this. I have no doubt about that.

When I reach the bottom of the pile, I find a note in the handwriting I was expecting to find in the box.

Now the debt's over two million.
I own you.
Feel free to tattoo that on your ass,
just so there's no confusion in your mind.

That smug asshole.

I'm going to kill him.

I yank open the nightstand drawer, but the lockbox where I keep the gun is gone.

Mount.

No matter what happens in my life, it seems, the answer lately is *Mount*.

Someone bangs on my apartment door, and I stalk toward it.

Go down fighting or die trying. That's how I walked into this, and that's how I'm going to end it.

I flip the dead bolts and fling open the door, but it's

not Mount outside.

"I've missed you, Keira. I hear you haven't been missing me."

I blink twice, unable to comprehend the fact that my dead husband is standing in front of me—very much alive—before everything goes black.

Mount and Keira's story continues in

DEFIANT QUEEN

ALSO BY MEGHAN MARCH

Take Me Back

Bad Judgment

BENEATH SERIES:
Beneath These Shadows
Beneath This Mask
Beneath This Ink
Beneath These Chains
Beneath These Scars
Beneath These Lies
Beneath the Truth

DIRTY BILLIONAIRE TRILOGY:
Dirty Billionaire
Dirty Pleasures
Dirty Together

AUTHOR'S NOTE

UNAPOLOGETICALLY SEXY ROMANCE

I'd love to hear from you. Connect with me at:

Website: www.meghanmarch.com
Facebook: www.facebook.com/MeghanMarchAuthor
Twitter: www.twitter.com/meghan_march
Instagram: www.instagram.com/meghanmarch

ABOUT THE AUTHOR

Meghan March has been known to wear camo face paint and tromp around in the woods wearing mud-covered boots, all while sporting a perfect manicure. She's also impulsive, easily entertained, and absolutely unapologetic about the fact that she loves to read and write smut.

Her past lives include slinging auto parts, selling lingerie, making custom jewelry, and practicing corporate law. Writing books about dirty-talking alpha males and the strong, sassy women who bring them to their knees is by far the most fabulous job she's ever had.

She loves hearing from her readers at meghanmarchbooks@gmail.com.

60710797R00149

Made in the USA
Middletown, DE
03 January 2018